Perilous and Beautiful

A Novel

Patricia Lucia

Noble Light Press

First Paperback edition March 2023

Cover design By Ashe Rodrigues

ISBN 978-0-578-87339-8 (Paperback)

ISBN 979-8-218-00667-9 (ebook)

Published by Noble Light Press

Pattiluciawrites.com

To all the souls —seen and unseen—
who graced a little cafe and its owner
with their love and friendship

Perilous and Beautiful

Chapter 1

When Marabella left the city three months after the Towers came down, Bear walked through Inwood Park along the path they had once jogged. She paused by the inlet where they had fed bagels to the ducks and to a solitary swan. Farther up the path she paused under the crisscross lattice of the railway bridge, her memory filled with the image of Marabella pointing her camera toward the architectural structure stretching out across the waterway. And when the path led her to the top of the wooded hill overlooking the Hudson, Bear stepped off the path and walked to the rock ledge, hidden from view, where they had often sat to watch the sunset. She lingered here, her mind returning to chilly autumn afternoons just like this one, when they had reclined on the smooth surface of the ledge, sweaty and elated after a run. Here, with the Hudson River spread out before them and the tall, thick trees of Inwood Park at their backs, Marabella had kissed her.

She sat down on the ledge and let a flood of memory return. In the months before the kiss, she had been reserved but friendly in all their interactions, professional in their conversations in the teacher's lounge and respectful of Marabella's devotion to her Seventh-Day Adventist faith. She had not given, as far as she could tell, a single outward hint of attraction to her coworker. This had not been easy. It felt far more natural for her to smile when Marabella entered a room, for her cheeks to flush when Marabella greeted her in the hallway or spoke to her across the lunch table. She found Marabella's beauty stunning and sometimes smiled to herself about how literally she meant that. Bear did feel quite stunned in her presence.

Marabella was like a living watercolor painting. Her deep brown, thought-filled eyes reminded Bear of a Chagall self-portrait that had drawn her into the painter's eyes and held her there, wanting to know their language. Marcella's cheekbones and lips, a perfect symmetry, were accented playfully by the mischievous mole on the right side of her chin. Her smile hinted at a secret world she inhabited and the possibility of an invitation there; it gave Bear the same unmoored feeling of floating on the whimsy of Chagall.

Marabella's presence in the teacher's lounge was highlighted by her beauty, of which she seemed completely unaware, and by her quiet attentiveness. Marabella was not chatty. This alone stood out in a room full of chattering, commiserating, and often gossiping teachers. So when Marabella spoke—in English if Bear was present—Bear listened carefully to every word and sometimes nodded. She said very little herself, in the beginning. She was, after all, a stranger in a foreign land.

Bear had just arrived in the city, and IS 52, which was located one block from the 200th Street stop on the A train, was her first official teaching job. She could have stayed in Massachusetts after passing her licensure exam, but she wanted to get as far away as she could from those places that had never wanted her anyway, and her new teaching license was good in almost every state. It was her ticket out. When she heard New York was recruiting thousands of new teachers, Bear took the Amtrak into the city for a job fair and returned with an offer of employment from District 6 in Manhattan.

She found a little one-bedroom apartment on Seaman Avenue, across from the entrance to Inwood Park, where the tennis and racquetball courts echoed with shouts and the thwap of rackets; where the squeals of children filled the play area in which they climbed, slid, and swung; and where a small fountain sent up streams of water, inviting the patter of their little feet through the puddles. She moved in on Labor Day weekend, when the park teemed with picnickers, baseball and soccer players, and every parking spot in front of her building was taken. Beth, Bear's sister, double-parked her husband's SUV and waited in the car while Bear brought in her boxes, an inflatable mattress, and finally, tenderly, the small rosemary plant Nonna had given her.

"This is madness," Beth had said, watching the throngs of people cross in front of the car and pour through the park entrance. Bear had laughed. She breathed in the park air, a mix of cut grass and burning charcoal, the aroma from a hot dog stand, and a whiff of weed. She felt the chaotic energy of the city seeping into her skin, and she liked it.

"It may seem like madness to you," she had said, "but this is my new life."

Weeks later, Bear sat in the teacher's lounge of IS 52, eating a tuna sandwich from her brown-bag lunch and listening to the banter of the other teachers, who mostly spoke in Spanish. Marabella had

Perilous and Beautiful

entered and exchanged greetings with them in
Spanish, then found an empty seat across from her.

"I love the smell of autumn," Marabella said after
a moment. Bear had been studying the bread crust
on her tuna sandwich in order to avoid staring at
Marabella and now looked up, surprised, partly because Marabella was looking directly into her eyes
and partly because Marabella had just said something she had often thought but rarely said aloud,
especially to a stranger.

"And the leaves are starting to turn in Inwood
Park," Marabella was saying. Bear nodded, embarrassed that she had not been inside the park yet
even though she lived across the street. She had
been too busy settling into her new place, which at
the moment was barely furnished.

"Have you been there?" asked Marabella.

"I just moved in across the street."

"On Seaman?"

"Yes!"

"The building with the mural of the Manhattan
tribe in the lobby?

"Yes," said Bear. "It's very beautiful."

Something stirred behind Marabella's eyes when
Bear said this and her smile became a warm flicker.

"I'm Marabella, by the way."

11

"I'm Adelina, but my friends call me Bear."

Marabella raised a brow. "Bear?"

"*Orsa* in Italian," said Bear. "My nonna gave me that name."

Marabella nodded, conscious that the other women around the lunch table had stopped talking and now glanced in their direction.

"May I call you Orsa?"

The following Sunday, Marabella gave Bear a tour of Inwood Park and they went on their first run.

"This is where Manhattan was sold," she said and pointed to a large plaque by an even larger area, where the trunk of a majestic tree had been rooted. "Right under the tree that stood here." Bear lingered by the plaque, less interested in what it said than in her desire to picture life beneath such a tree and all the memories it must have held. *Trees hold the memories and wisdom of the land,* Nonna had once said. *If we listen close enough, they will share it.*

Marabella appointed herself Bear's tour guide to the city—a role she seemed delighted to fill—showing her a new site every Sunday. Not Saturdays, she explained, because that was her Sabbath. During the week, they ran in the park after school, changing in the staff bathroom and stuffing their clothes into their backpacks. Marabella never asked about Bear's past but shared that she had been married once before, when she was eighteen. It had lasted only a year.

"He was cruel," Marabella had said when Bear asked why. She added that the cruelty she endured in that brief marriage had given her reprieve from any pressure to marry again, at least for a while. She had looked at Bear directly when she said this, as if her words held hidden meaning.

Bear pushed aside any thought of romance between them, even when Marabella seemed to send mixed messages. So grateful was she to have a friend in New York that the thought of doing anything to jeopardize it was terrifying. So their friendship deepened with the hues of autumn in Inward Park, and each Sunday they visited a place on Marabella's list of 'Things Orsa Must See in New York.'

Bear was giddy as a child on these adventures, marveling at the dark blur of the A train tunnel between 125th Street and 59th as the car rocked and the steel wheels screeched. She drank in the cacophony of scent and sound on the New York streets, savored knishes with mustard from street vendors, took in the New York skyline from the Staten Island Ferry, and squeezed her eyes shut on the elevator to the top of the Empire State Building.

When Marabella took her to the World Trade Center, Bear stood on the sidewalk under Tower 1 and gasped at the enormity of its base, a perimeter that took an entire city block. She looked up dizzily at the giant steel towers, which stood like twin titan lighthouses, reflecting the sun in all directions as far as the eye could see, as steadfast as the north star in Ursa Minor.

She had found her home. Somehow, in the chaos and bustle of New York City, the Towers anchored and assured her. She could put down roots here. Find love and a new family. It was all possible under the twinkling glint of the Towers.

Marabella had kissed her on a chilly, gray afternoon in early November. The bright yellow leaves of the tulip trees and the red leaves of the oaks had long fallen and turned brown, and the trees' bare crowns stretched upward toward the approaching winter as if to ask for mercy. But Bear felt only the warmth of Marabella's lips and the certainty of Marabella's hand as it guided Bear to her warm, soft breasts. If there had been any warning in the trees or on the wind, in the gray clouds above them or in the clandestine nature of the kiss itself, Bear had turned from it. She saw only the invitation in Marabella's eyes to the secret world she had wanted to enter since the first time Marabella had looked at her from across the lunch table.

She had leaned toward Bear at first and reached for the silver chain around Bear's neck that held Nonna's ring.

"I've been wanting to ask you about this," she said.

"My nonna gave it to me when I graduated from high school," Bear said.

"Why do you wear it around your neck?"

"It's a little small for me, and . . ."

Bear hesitated, and Marabella's eyes felt like they bored into her thoughts. "I wanted to give it to someone special one day." Bear had known what this meant. She knew that, even though she had not said it out loud, Marabella would know she was waiting to fall in love with a woman.

Marabella nodded. "You're looking for your beloved."

"Yes. My family."

"In this big, crazy city," Marabella had said and shook her head, a grin lifting a corner of her mouth.

"Seemed as good a place as any."

And that's when Marabella had kissed her, had taken her hand and moved it under her jacket to her warm heart and breast, had pressed Bear against the stone beneath them, her dark hair falling all around Bear's closed eyes. And Bear had given herself fully to the kiss, thrown off all fear of a squandered friendship and boarded Marabella's train, now speeding through the darkness to her secret world.

At one point, Marabella broke away from their kiss.

"I can't be that for you," she said.

"Be what?"

"Your beloved," she said, resisting the approach of Bear's mouth. "You have to understand that."

"OK," whispered Bear, lost in the deep, rich earth of Marabella's eyes.

"Say you understand that, Orsa," she said, resting her fingers on Bear's chin.

"I understand."

Bear hadn't known she was lying. She only knew the touch of Marabella's skin, the smell of her hair, the sound of her quickened breath, the welcome weight of her body. They made love for the first time on the hard, cold stone, oblivious to its hardness and to the cold; oblivious to the swirling dead leaves all around them and the darkening currents of the Hudson River below.

Now Bear lay back on the ledge, pushed her hands into her peacoat pockets and pulled out her phone. She had a missed call from Ronnie and a text. *I'm worried about you. Are you all right?* Ronnie had no idea she was here, in Inwood Park, sitting on a rock she had once shared with Marabella, where they had once kissed and made love. Ronnie had no idea about a lot of things.

She closed her eyes and thought about the approaching holidays and remembered how lonely holidays had been before Marabella. They were for family, after all, and Bear didn't have a passport to that country anymore. Family, like any country, had borders and boundaries. Bear was an exile.

Joy had returned to the holidays with Marabella, even if they could not spend as much time together as Bear would have liked. Still, they had laughed and sung all the way to Bear's apartment that first Christmas, carrying a tree on their shoulders, and had decorated it with angels. Bear loved the angel theme so much that they added more angels each year, until the last Christmas when Marabella had begun to turn away and a cloud of gray dread formed over the tree and cast a shadow over the painted smiles of the angels.

Even now Bear grimaced at her mistake. She had known the rules of Marabella's secret world. Secret worlds must have their rules. She had agreed to the lies and cover-ups, refraining from public displays of affection in the city, even when they walked

17

along Christopher Street; agreeing to the story that their vacation in Provincetown was 'a trip to Boston with a group of teachers.' Even the pictures they had taken in Provincetown—playing Scrabble on Herring Cove Beach, whale-watching on the *Portuguese Princess*, the hot tub at Gabriel's Inn—had to be hidden away.

Bear's mistake happened one morning during their third autumn, when they walked under the golden canopy of leaves in Inwood Park. She had known the foolishness of it, much like one who runs into a burning building knows the risk of calamity but also knows that what might be saved or retrieved is worth such a risk. What was she saving or retrieving? It was their very relationship, she thought, trapped inside a burning building whose flames were closing in all around them. The only way it could survive was to escape. Perhaps her mistake was not that she had run into the flames, but that she had been the only one who had felt their heat and sensed the urgency, the desperation, to run from them.

The morning felt full of promise with the sunlight glowing in the leaves above, and Bear had taken Nonna's ring from its chain and put it in her pocket. When she was sure they were alone on the path, she stopped and touched Marabella's hand, then knelt in the leaves. And, extending Nonna's ring, Bear had asked Marabella to marry her, then watched helplessly as a shadow crossed Marabella's eyes.

"Orsa," she began softly, and lifted Bear to her feet. "You know I can't be that for you. I can't be your beloved."

Bear had pressed her lips together and returned the ring to her pocket. She had known, yet she had not known. She had understood this and had not. Marabella loved her, she knew it, and Bear had believed that this alone could rewrite their story.

She was wrong.

"You're my beloved to me, Bella," she had murmured and they walked on in silence, warm tears rolling down her chilled face. Marabella turned away, sniffling softly, and pointed her camera at the changing leaves of a tulip tree.

Distance grew between them in the days and weeks that followed. It was a distance made of sadness, of endings and of futile yearnings. Marabella did not come on Christmas night, as she had before, to curl up in Bear's arms on the sofa and kiss in the glow of the angel tree, and the Christmas cookies Bear had baked that afternoon—Marabella's favorite—sat uncovered and hardening on the kitchen table.

This was the end, the inevitable end Marabella had warned her about on the day they had first kissed. The end Bear had said she understood. Of all the lies she had told or had helped to tell with Marabella, this had been the biggest and the most crushing.

Bear didn't know how long she had been lying on the ledge. She opened her eyes to a twilit sky and the buzzing of the phone in her pocket.

"Hey, where are you?" Ronnie asked. "I brought dinner."

"I'm not far," said Bear. She didn't want to tell Ronnie she was in the park just across the street. She wasn't quite ready to come home.

"How are you feeling?"

"OK, I guess."

"Did you talk to your therapist?"

"I'm fine, Ronnie. Really."

"You feeling anxious today?"

"Yeah, me and eight million other people."

Ronnie was silent for a moment.

"You feel like Italian?" she asked. "I got Italian."

"I *am* Italian," Bear said, aware that her words had sharp edges and that she held them like a knife to create a safe distance. Ronnie didn't seem to pick up on that.

She laughed. "There's my girl," she said. "See you soon."

Bear lay back down and peered at the first twinkling stars in the evening sky. Sounds of jazz music drifted up from the Hudson below as a Circle Line Sunset Cruise rounded the northern end of Manhattan and traveled south toward the George Washington Bridge. She recalled the F-16s that flew low over the GW the day the Towers came down, and the smell of those smoldering titans, her exploded north star, hanging like a cloud of despair over the city.

She had not seen Marabella for almost a year when the Towers came down. They had both moved on in their own ways: Marabella with a man from her church and Bear with Ronnie, whom she had met through Elite Dating, a new online dating site. All professionals. All screened. Nothing messy or complicated.

Bear had gone through her own stages of grief over Marabella. In the angry, one-night-stand stage, she had once drunk-dialed Marabella from a bar while her date was in the bathroom. During her bargaining and begging stage, Bear wrote a letter to Marabella, insisting that she would be perfectly fine with seeing her just once a year. And during her depressed and anxious night-walker stage, Bear paced the neighborhood, past midnight most nights, and if she was anxious enough, she ran. In the end she arrived at acceptance. Mostly.

She had been a fool. Maybe it was the *in love* part that had made her a fool, she concluded. Maybe it was time for an age of reason. So Bear put away all notions of falling in love again and erected the gates of reason around her heart. And through those gates walked Ronnie.

Bear hadn't expected to feel this way about Marabella leaving the city. She would have taken it better if the Towers were still standing. They had been her anchor, her compass. Marabella had been her family. It didn't matter that Marabella didn't see it that way. She had *felt* like family, and Bear had found comfort in knowing Marabella still lived in the same city, under the same stars, breathing the same air, watching the same clouds.

But now she was gone. Packed up and moved to Hialeah with her fiancé and her whole family. Every time Bear thought about it—the Towers and Marabella both gone—she got that floaty feeling in her head and stomach. It was not the good kind of floaty feeling, like when she first met Marabella. It was terrifying, like she had no roots—or anchor or home or family. Like she didn't belong anywhere.

22

That's how she had felt most of the day after Marabella had called from somewhere in New Jersey, driving her packed car south on 95. Marabella must have heard the crack in Bear's voice.

"We're all going to be OK, Orsa," she said. "*Tranquila.*"

"OK," Bear said and held the phone like a lifeline to her ear, wanting to hold the sound of Marabella's breath. She heard instead the loud hum of highway traffic.

"Remember me whenever you hear k. d. lang or Luis Miguel, OK?"

Bear winced. She remembered the first time Marabella had played k. d. lang's "Constant Craving" for her, and how she had called Bear her *little Italian kd lang with green eyes*. Then she made Bear read every word of the lyrics as if they held secret codes. Bear closed her eyes to the memory of dancing to "Hasta Que Me Olvides" in her living room, and how tightly Marabella had held her when she sang the chorus.

"OK," Bear said again. She wanted to tell Marabella she loved her. "Be safe out there, Bella," she said instead. "It's a wild world."

And so, Marabella left the city with her family after the Towers came down. And took Bear's family with her too.

A shiver ran through Bear's body as she rose from the ledge and stood to gaze out across the dark Hudson toward New Jersey. Somewhere in her line of vision Marabella drove into her new life, away from the dust and heartbreak of a shattered city. Bear turned and walked along the path, under the railroad bridge and along the inlet, which reflected soft pools of light from the streetlamps. A new thought formed and brought with it a tremor that quickened her heart and her step. She walked faster now with a sense of urgency, her breath in puffs, disappearing behind her. This was not her home anymore, she thought. She had no roots. She did not belong here. The row of buildings along Seaman Avenue rose up ahead as she exited the park, and more terrifying thoughts began to swirl. This wasn't a place of endless possibility, she thought. It was a prison. A prison from which she needed to escape.

Bear entered the building and glanced at the mural of the Manhattan tribe behind the artificial blinking Christmas tree that decorated the lobby every year. The Christmas lights and decorations that had given such cheer before now poked at the sickening panic that grew in her gut.

She mounted the stairs to her apartment and thought of the woman waiting for her, who was still, mostly, a stranger. A woman who didn't understand the irony of buying Italian takeout for an Italian girlfriend who had grown up in the kitchen with her nonna. Who thought her girlfriend should get on medication as soon as the Towers came down. A woman who had called the rosemary plant in her kitchen window 'quaint.' Yet, still, this was a woman who had left her condo in Boca to fly to New York two weeks after the Towers had come down. Who had shifted their long-distance relationship to a "let's live together a while and figure this out" kind of relationship. Bear paused at the door before taking out her key. Right now the only thing she wanted to figure out was how to get the hell out of this city.

Chapter 2

2008
Boca Raton, Florida

Bear sped east on Second Avenue toward Federal Road and checked her eyes in the rearview mirror for any hint that she had been crying. She groaned out loud when the light on the corner turned red. She was already late for a two o'clock appointment to see a commercial space on Federal. It was a space she hadn't wanted to see in the first place, but Ronnie had insisted. Bear argued that the place was too expensive for a coffeehouse start-up. Ronnie had countered with the veiled threat that if they weren't going to open their café in Boca, her preferred location, they had better find a really nice space somewhere else.

Most decisions arrived this way, like judgments meted out in a courtroom, awarded to the one with most will and wit. Like their decision to move to Florida. Bear hadn't wanted to move to Florida, least of all to Boca Raton, but Ronnie argued that she couldn't possibly know for sure until she visited, and once she had a taste of Boca, Ronnie said, she would never want to leave.

"Do I look like a Boca babe to you?" Bear had retorted.

"If you cleaned up a bit, maybe." Ronnie had smiled as if joking, but Bear knew better. And she knew she couldn't win the argument if she had never been to Florida, so she went.

Bear had felt a strange panic crawl up her neck as she boarded the plane and took her seat next to Ronnie. The last time she had been in a plane was before the Towers came down. A vacation flight to Boston with Marabella. From Boston, they had flown Cape Air, a six-seat Cessna, to Provincetown. Marabella had held Bear's hand tightly on each takeoff and landing, and Bear had loved being above the clouds with her. The clouds seemed like the safest and most natural place for them.

So why did she feel so panicked now? Bear wondered. Maybe it was another irrational fear that had crept in since the Towers, like her fear of subways. She had once loved riding the A train, especially on adventures with Marabella. Now she avoided them completely, no longer able to tolerate being underground without a way to escape. She took the bus instead, and often the bus took her to a therapist on the Lower East Side.

Maybe the panic was about Ronnie. The first year of their relationship had been punctuated by starts and stops, on-agains and off-agains. One year after Ronnie had moved into Bear's apartment on Seaman, Bear had returned the ridiculous ring Ronnie had given her—three diamonds set in a platinum band—and Ronnie had returned to Boca. Days later the phone calls began, and Bear's resolve melted like spring snow into the fertile soil of self-doubt. Her sister, Beth, called first.

"I just don't get it, Bear," she said. "Ronnie's the best thing that's happened to you. She's smart and pretty; she has a great job; everyone loves her. Even Mom loves her!"

Bear felt the same dizziness on these calls as she did in arguments with Ronnie. Her thoughts clouded and her words garbled. Yes, she agreed, Ronnie was smart, and she was pretty by her family's standards: tall, blonde, and blue-eyed. Yet in the darkened and quieted acre of Bear's interior, she shook her head in protest. No one was more beautiful than

Marabella in this secret place, where her heart had once opened wide and run wild and free. Where beauty lay in autumn leaves and in a mother whale nuzzling her calf, in sunsets from a ledge overlooking the Hudson and in a solitary swan in the Inwood Park inlet. Where she could watch Marabella sip chicken soup from a spoon at the Riverdale Diner and think it was the most beautiful thing in the world. Marabella was, for Bear, the best thing that had ever happened to her, and losing Marabella had created a valley of shadows, a fallow acre haunted by the ghosts of pastoral beauty and love, while above, under the metallic light of her churning, rational days, Ronnie had arrived on frequent flyer miles with credentials and a passport to that country from which Bear had long been exiled.

Bear managed the flight with a steady stream of rum and Coke, and, as the plane descended over Fort Lauderdale, she marveled at the ropes of pink and blue neon lights that decorated the tops of the tallest buildings. Farther south, the lights of Miami glowed in the night sky, where Bear imagined Marabella putting her children to bed.

The next day Bear sat on Juno Beach with her feet sunk in the sand, and listened to the waves gently slap the shore. Ronnie had stayed in the car to answer a call, and Bear was relieved to be alone. Her thoughts returned to the phone call she had

had with Nonna a few days before. Nonna had never expressed approval or disapproval of Ronnie, but mostly remained silent and listened.

"Sometimes I don't know why I'm with her, Nonna," Bear had said.

"Some relationships are like places," Nonna said after a moment. "They are a whole world unto themselves."

Bear had nodded. That was how it felt with Marabella. Nonna must have known that. "Yes."

"And some relationships," Nonna continued, "are like trains. They transport us between possibilities."

Though Bear didn't fully understand what Nonna was saying, she knew better than to ask for an explanation. She had to figure it out for herself. Nonna's words settled on her skin and mingled with the warmth of the sun. She breathed in the sea air, and the breeze brushed her face like fingers. It was settled then, she thought. She would come to Florida, and she would discover all the reasons why. Eventually.

When the New York public schools let out for summer in 2004, they packed up Bear's apartment on Seaman Avenue and moved to Ronnie's old condo. A prolonged debate over where to buy a house in Florida began shortly after their arrival and ended with Ronnie's deposit on a house in Boca, just a few streets north of Mizner Park. Bear had preferred the humbler seaside towns that lay north of Boca; towns that had a funky, bohemian, beachy vibe, like Lake Worth; but selling the idea to Ronnie had proved impossible.

"There are a lot of lesbian couples in Lake Worth," she said one Sunday morning as Ronnie scrolled through listings online. Bear imagined living on one of the town's narrow neighborhood streets and making new friends whose homes she could walk to if invited. Ronnie had laughed without looking away from the screen.

"And gangs and drugs and crime," she countered.

"Have you seen the adorable cottages there?"

"Little wood-framed things that can blow away in a hurricane."

"It's got a cute downtown . . ."

"Dive bars and trinket shops."

"And a small independent film theater," Bear said, thinking fondly of the times she had gone to the Angelika Film Center in the Village. This time Ronnie turned from the listings and faced Bear.

"You like independent films?" she asked in-credulously. Bear flinched and remembered her outings to the Angelika had been with Marabella, not Ronnie, then recovered with a shrug of feigned indifference.

"Sometimes."

Bear lost the argument for settling in Lake Worth, but two years later, when she had successfully made a case for opening a coffeehouse cafe, she set her sights again on the little town. Bear's business concept had been so unique that Ronnie could find no fault, no crack in her presentation.

"We could brand that," Ronnie had said. "And have multiple locations."

Bear had nodded and smiled, not because she felt vindicated by Ronnie or because she shared Ronnie's excitement about the monetary possibilities. She had just gained vital knowledge: what motivated Ronnie to support her idea. Bear herself cared little about branding and expansion. She had a different vision for the place, one that had more to do with Nonna than Ronnie would ever know.

Nonna had grown frail since Bear had moved to Florida and, after a fall, had been moved to a nursing home. Bear called every Sunday morning while on a long walk alone around the neighborhood.

"*Orsita!*" Nonna cried when she heard her voice. "How is my precious? Have you arrived at your new possibilities?"

Bear usually had little to offer for an answer. Her life with Ronnie remained isolated. She had a few work acquaintances at the high school but no real friends. She knew Ronnie's family, longtime equestrians in West Boca, and Ronnie's friends from the hospital where she worked. They were people she would not have chosen for her own friends, and none of them felt like family.

But as the business plans materialized, Bear brought her excitement to Nonna on her Sunday morning walks, and Nonna quietly hummed her delight. In their last conversation, Nonna spoke of trains again.

"Your train is approaching the station," she said, after Bear had described her search for just the right place for the café. "You will know when you see it."

"I'm going to make it the most beautiful place, Nonna."

"Yes," Nonna said. "And you will find new friends and new love there, Orsita, and remember, sometimes a beautiful place is also a train."

"I—I don't understand, Nonna," Bear had stammered. She didn't know which part was more perplexing, the 'new love' part or the train.

Nonna had laughed softly. "The most important thing to remember, precious, is how God and the angels see you. How they have always seen you. You are beautiful and perfect in every way, Orsita."

Bear didn't know why of all the times Nonna had said these words to her, this particular time made her cry. She was sure Nonna heard the crack in her voice when she said goodbye.

Three days later, Nonna was gone, and Bear went into silence, putting aside all business endeavors, all thoughts of the café. She spent most afternoons after school walking the soft sands of Spanish River Beach until the sun sank in the west.

During Bear's quiet mourning time, Ronnie had agreed to a Lake Worth location for the café. Maybe it was out of sympathy, or maybe she sensed a new determination growing in Bear, an imperceptible force that made Bear stand a bit taller, even in grief, and that deepened the set of her brow.

And so it was, on a particular Saturday afternoon in November, Bear raced east on Second Avenue in Lake Worth, having cried most of the way up 95 from Boca. She had just checked her eyes and thrown her crumpled tissue in the console when the light turned red, and caused her to slow down just enough to glance to her left, where a *For Rent* sign hung in the window of a tiny building under an enormous mango tree. Bear yanked her car into the small parking lot and in a moment had pulled out her phone and dialed the number. This was the place. She knew it.

Chapter 3

Three months later

Bear wiped a shine into the espresso machine and checked the register for one-dollar bills. In a few short hours, dozens of songwriters, poets, cross-dressing comedians, and their fans would occupy every square foot of Les Beans Café, violating the crap out of its occupancy limit and spilling out onto Second Avenue. Open mic nights had become, in the few short months since opening, a loud and colorful affirmation of Bear's leap-of-faith idea to open a quirky, beautiful café with a punny name, and her excitement on Thursdays usually tipped toward elation.

pun? Les Misérable

But not today.

Today she felt a growing lead snake in her gut, curling upward, shortening her breath and pushing her pulse into the back of her throat. Panic tingled across her scalp like a creeping centipede, and she thought of that unopened bottle of Prozac in the bottom of her backpack.

Bear took a deep breath and steadied herself just as the bell on the front door chimed and Linda, a curvaceous thirty-something, still dressed in her Saint Mary's Hospital scrubs, entered, all smiles.

"Bartender, please!" she sang. "Hook me up, love."

Bear forced a smile. "The usual?"

Linda's daily after-work flybys usually tickled Bear. She looked forward to Linda's snark and in-nuendo, even her confusing references to Dave Matthews songs. But today Bear needed more than banter. Today she could use a friend. Someone to ease the lead in her gut and the prickly panic at her temples. The truth was, she hardly knew Linda outside their lighthearted afternoon banter. And Linda hardly knew how much Bear needed a friend.

Bear pulled the triple shots and frothed the milk for Linda's latte in silence, noticing a slight tremble at the tips of her fingers.

"Coming to the open mic?" she asked finally. Linda's smiling face would give her some comfort at least. Bear wished she could say that to Linda without sounding crazy.

"Tell you what," said Linda, watching Bear's hands take her ten-dollar bill and work the register. "I'm going to go home, drink half of this latte, fill it back up with rum, get into something slutty, and *then* come back and cruise the shit out of Open Mic Night."

"That's very romantic," said Bear, attempting humor as she pressed her hands flat on the counter.

"Where's Ronnie?" Linda asked. "Isn't she supposed to be your work date on Thursdays?"

"California. She's working the Pride festival in San Diego this weekend."

"What the hell for?"

"Expansion, I guess. Something about franchising." Bear knew it sounded ridiculous.

Linda tilted her head and squinted. "Your girlfriend left you working alone so she could go to a networking event all the way across the country?"

"Yeah." Bear forced a toothy grin.

"With *this* crowd?"

"Yeah."

"K," Linda said, nodding like she had just received an order. "I'll be back."

"Yeah?"

"Heck yeah!" Linda chirped. "Gotta make the best of what's around, Bear Bear, and I'm around."

This time, Bear did not have to force a smile.

Les Beans Café was quiet as it was on most late afternoons. Adele sang "Hometown Glory" from the mixed CD Linda had given Bear, a CD with "Les Beans Mix" scrawled across the front. Two regulars lounged on the sofas with laptops. Bear moved around the room with a watering can, giving each floor plant and hanging plant a healthy drink. The light softened in the room and reflected the golden hue of twilight. She lit incense sticks and stuck them into the dirt of the floor plants, leaving silvery ribbons of smoke twisting upward through the fronds. She lit the candles that were sprinkled around the room.

To Bear, open mic nights were sacred gatherings, and so, every Thursday afternoon, she prepared the space with a sort of reverence for the creative souls who would enter under the brass bell.

Bear put the watering can away, took a deep breath and checked her phone. No text. No call. She had no idea what Ronnie was doing. She *did* know who she was doing it with, but that just made it worse.

Ronnie's argument for going to San Diego Pride had felt off from the beginning.

"We need to think about franchising," Ronnie had said.

"Isn't it a bit soon for that?" Bear asked. Les Beans Café had only been open for three months.

"Why are you always so negative?" Ronnie spouted in response.

"I'm just saying we've barely gotten this café off the ground," Bear said. *Was* she being negative? "Why not wait until—"

"There you go thinking small again," Ronnie interrupted. "We're never going to be successful with that attitude."

So Bear had dutifully printed out brochures for San Diego and ordered a display sign for Ronnie's booth. Still, she couldn't shake the suspicion that Ronnie's trip to San Diego had nothing to do with franchising their fledgling café.

Bear's doubts hadn't just crept up with the San Diego trip. Ronnie had stopped coming by the café after work and only showed up when it would be a disaster if she didn't. Like on open mic nights. Bear didn't mind running the place alone most of the time. Since she had quit her teaching job, the café had become her special creation, the canvas on which she painted every day with new and vibrant colors. But it was nearly impossible to keep up with the long line at the counter on open mic nights if she worked alone. Ronnie knew that. Even when she came to help on Thursdays, though, she seemed miserable, blaming her long hours in the cardiac care unit if Bear asked what was wrong. She came home later from work, too, often after Bear had closed the café and gone to bed. Letting off a little steam with the girls, she would say.

Then she had gotten that tattoo.

"You got a tattoo?" Bear said one morning in bed, when she glimpsed Ronnie's lower back and the three Chinese characters freshly inked there.

"So?" Ronnie had said.

"What does it mean?"

"Good health," Ronnie said, and rolled out of bed quickly to head for the shower.

And now there was San Diego. When Ronnie had come to the café at lunchtime to tell her she was catching a flight, Bear had been stunned. It was Thursday, after all. Open Mic Night. And the Pride presentation was on Saturday.

"What? You're leaving *now*?"

"I'm flying out in an hour."

"Why?"

"I have to get prepared, Adelina!" Ronnie exclaimed. She had never called Bear by the name Nonna had given her, and when she felt annoyed or impatient, she placed a special emphasis on the name only she used. *Adelina.* "Don't you understand what it takes to make a professional presentation?"

Bear was speechless. Nothing about this made sense.

"But how could you understand?" Ronnie continued. "Before this, you taught grammar to fifteen-year-olds."

This stung as it always did when Ronnie thought it necessary to remind Bear of how things worked in the *real world*. A physician's assistant in a cardiac care unit had far more responsibility than an English teacher in a B school. Real lives were at stake. What had been at stake in Bear's ghetto classroom, as Ronnie called it? Nouns and verbs?

Ronnie had acquired a list of questions for whenever Bear needed a reminder.

Who made it possible for you to own a home in Boca?

Who made it possible for you to have a business?

Who got you out of that shitty neighborhood in New York?

Eventually, her upbraiding would conclude with a real-time example of Bear's lack of motivation. Her car.

And after all the things I've done for you, you still drive around in that ridiculous Mercury Tracer Wagon.

"I *like* my car," Bear sometimes replied. "It's a real attention-getter at the Town Center Mall." It was true. Her Tracer—bought for a song when they moved to Florida—turned heads when she drove along US 1 and Glades Avenue. This tickled Bear. She couldn't deny it; the car had character.

When it came to her car, she wouldn't let Ronnie push her down. There were other lines Ronnie couldn't cross either. Ever. One line was Marabella; the other, Nonna. It had only taken once for Ronnie to know better.

Thank God you got away from that ditsy Dominican girlfriend who didn't even love you enough to come out, she said one day. *What a waste!*

The memory of her own reaction still frightened Bear. How quickly she had hurled the phone in Ronnie's direction, denting the wall a few feet from her head. Marabella was that shard of glass deep under Bear's skin, healed on the surface but sharp enough to cut an artery with the slightest pressure.

When Nonna had died in October and Ronnie suggested Bear stop using the name her grandmother had given her, Bear had gone silent in their relationship for nearly a month and refused to share meals or a bed with her. This looked like an extended tantrum to Ronnie, but in truth it was mostly grief. The silence and distance gave Bear the solitude she needed to mourn the only person in the world who had ever told her she was perfect just the way she was.

Ronnie was traveling to San Diego with Isabel. *My work wife*, Ronnie called her. Isabel understood the pressure of cardiac intensive care. Isabel was funny and smart. She spoke Mandarin and owned a condo on Palm Beach Island. Most of all, Isabel worshiped Ronnie.

Bear saw this in the way Isabel looked at Ronnie when she visited their home. She saw it in the way Isabel leaped up when Ronnie needed a refill or nosh. She saw it in the way Isabel laughed a little too loudly at Ronnie's biting sarcasm.

Once, after an uncomfortable Sunday afternoon barbecue, Bear confronted Ronnie about Isabel.

"You're insecure," Ronnie had said. "Maybe you should put a little more effort into getting to know Isabel instead of being jealous of her."

Was she jealous? Bear wondered. Was she overreacting?

"I just haven't been feeling that great about *us*, I guess," she said finally. "I mostly feel sad."

Ronnie gaslighting?

45

If Bear had been completely honest, she might have said she felt sad about all the choices she'd made since New York. All the things she had thought she needed. The house. The pool. The manicured yard. The impressive zip code. A partner her family finally accepted.

If she had been completely honest, she would have said she was sad about her choice not to fly to Massachusetts for Nonna's funeral. And sad about the crushing thought of Nonna dying alone in that nursing home.

"Baby, listen." Ronnie spoke more softly than she had in a long time. "Maybe you should see the doctor. It sounds like you might be a little depressed." She kissed her forehead. "You know what I say," she said with a grin. "Better living through chemistry." She tucked a strand of Bear's hair behind her ear. "I'm sure the doctor can give you something to smooth out those edges."

Ronnie's tenderness felt like a cool glass of water on a hot afternoon. Maybe she was right. Bear made an appointment with her GP the next day.

"I think I'm having mood swings," she told Dr. Gomez.

"Any other concerns?" the doctor asked.

"My partner thinks I'm a little depressed."

"What do you think?"

"I don't know."

Dr. Gomez gave Bear a prescription for ten milligrams of Prozac.

"Try this and let me know if it relieves you."

Bear had filled the prescription but left the bottle in her backpack. When Ronnie asked, Bear assured her that she was taking them and feeling much better.

"I'm proud of you," Ronnie said. "You can just be a little sensitive sometimes."

At 7:00, the place had already begun to buzz. A line had formed at the counter when Bear noticed Linda weaving through the throng toward her.

"Excuse me, excuse me," Linda was saying. "We're the help. Coming through!"

We? Bear thought, then noticed Linda pulling someone along behind her. All Bear could see was spiky, red hair, the color of a robin's breast.

Linda was all business. "Bear, this is Sophie. Sophie, Bear. I thought we could take orders and names for the people in line."

"Sounds great!" Bear exclaimed. "Thank you!"

She looked at Sophie, who stood still and scanned the room. Bear followed her gaze over the freshly painted cream walls; the colorful local art; the thrift-shop chandeliers hung whimsically across the ceiling; the old leather sofas in the corner around a coffee table; the softly lit lamps on end tables; and the small stage where silky, burgundy fabric hung from ceiling to floor, pulled back like drapes to display the painted logo on the back wall, a silhouette of two women under a full moon, heads bent toward each other as if to whisper or to kiss.

"It's very nice to meet you, Sophie," Bear said after a moment.

Sophie's gaze moved slowly from the stage wall's silhouette to Bear. In a tone barely audible above the din, she said, "You have a very beautiful place." Linda put a pad of paper and a pen in Sophie's hand and guided her back to the end of the line.

"Put their name at the top of the ticket and number it. Let them know we'll call them when their drinks are ready," she instructed over the noise.

Bear smiled at Linda's can-do attitude and Sophie's willingness to spend her first date with Linda in the weeds at a café. *That's promising*, Bear thought. Linda hadn't mentioned having a date, though.

Micki, otherwise known as the Worm Queen, arrived at seven to set up the performers. Micki had just the right amount of charisma and weirdness to be a perfect emcee for open mics. She owned a vermiculture start-up and always had a worm story to share because, as she put it, "The best stories are the ones that make you squirm." Micki wore her signature red high-top Converse and her "magic" hat, a straw fedora. She swore that if she didn't wear it, the whole evening might go to shit. Which wouldn't be so bad, she'd add with a shrug, because if it was *worm* shit, she could sell it at a damn good price.

Micki put out a large, clear vase with "Tips, Please!" printed across the front in bubble letters, and placed a five-dollar-bill inside. She found the broom and, holding the bristles, pointed the end of the stick carefully to a power strip on the ceiling, where the two stage lights were plugged in. She tapped the switch and the small stage lit up, high-lighting the burgundy curtains and the café logo, and glinting off the microphone stand, which stood by a stool on an oriental rug.

Micki took the sign-up sheet from the table by the door and made her way to the counter.

"We've got fourteen performances tonight, Bear," she said, "mostly music, a couple of poets, and Steve with his comedy routine."

"Perfect!" Bear replied. At seven minutes for each performance, they could keep the evening to just under two hours. She poured milk into a small pitcher and held it under the steam wand. "Cappuccino?"

"Yes, please!" Micki replied. "It's eight o'clock. I'm gonna get this party started!"

Micki dimmed the room lights and, smiling broadly, stepped under the island of light on stage, placing her cappuccino carefully on the stool before turning back to the crowd.

"Good evening and welcome to open mic night at Les Beans Café, the most magical night of the week!"

The room erupted in whoops and applause.

"And every one of you, the songwriters, the poets and comedians, and the folks who have come out to support your friends, all of you—yes, you!" Micki pointed to a young man on the sofa who had gestured *Me?* "All of you make this night so special. So give yourselves a round of applause for being awesome!"

Bear took a moment to look around the room. Every seat was filled, and it seemed every Mexican tile in the floor had someone standing on it. It was hard to believe she had created this, even harder to believe she had gotten the help she needed to get through the night without Ronnie. Linda and Sophie moved from behind the counter into the room with iced coffees, smoothies, and lattes. *They look like they're having fun, too*, thought Bear.

At halftime, Micki took a moment, as she always did, for a commercial break.

"And now a word from our sponsor!" She held a bag of coffee in each hand. "Your favorite coffee, Les Beans Coffee, is made with orgasmically organic beans, grown with no pesticides or chemical fertilizers. And do you know what that means?

"What?" asked several voices.

"These farmers probably use worm fertilizer! The cleanest and best fertilizer in the world!" Laughter rippled through the room. "Les Beans Coffee is slow-roasted in small batches to bring out the very best flavor in the beans. Do you know what that means?"

"What?"

"We have the tastiest beans in the world!" she exclaimed with a wink to even more laughter. "So bring some Les Beans home with you tonight. We have Ethiopia Sophie, a smooth single-origin with notes of honeysuckle and dark chocolate... or maybe you would prefer Sumatra Momma. She's earthy and full-bodied. Complex and sweet."

"Oh, yeah!" someone shouted.

"So bring home your favorite Les Beans!" Micki shouted, holding both bags over her head. "We'll even grind them for you!" she added to whoops and hollers.

After the last performance, a duet with Jake on guitar and his girlfriend, Lyndsey, on viola, Micki invited Bear to the stage as she always did to say good night. Bear felt her phone vibrate, took a quick glance, and put it back in her pocket. Three missed calls from Ronnie. A little late for concern, she thought, and stepped onto the stage.

"I'd like to thank you all for coming out tonight and making it such a memorable night for all of us," Bear began. "This is a little stage, but it takes a lot of courage to get up here, so I'd like to give a special thank-you to all of our performers, poets, and comedians. And, until next time, as you move through your week and as you face whatever challenges may come your way, please remember how the creator sees you, always..." Bear paused and looked around the room. The open mic regulars knew what was coming and fell silent. "Always remember that you are all so beautiful and so perfect in every way. Thank you for coming out. Have a good night."

"Afterparty?"

Linda's words poked Bear out of her thoughts. The three of them, Bear, Linda, and Sophie, had moved through the empty coffeehouse, tidying and putting up chairs. They had locked the doors, wiped down tables, and swept the floors. Bear still had her hands in the warm dishwater when Linda stepped into the kitchen.

"Let's hang out a little," Linda pressed. "I've got a bottle of wine in the car."

"Sounds wonderful," Bear said, pulling the stopper in the sink and wiping her hands on her apron. She pulled her phone out of her apron pocket and checked for messages.

What's going on? Call me! Ronnie's text read.

"You sure?" asked Linda, eyeing Bear's phone.

Bear turned off her phone and stuck it in the side pocket of her backpack in the corner of the kitchen.

"Yes," she said. "I'd love to."

Chapter 4

"So it's intermission, and I'm standing outside the Bamboo Room having a smoke when I see this one." Linda gestured with her coffee mug, half filled with wine, toward Sophie. "She's sitting on the curb finishing off a whole bottle of wine by herself."

"I had my reasons," Sophie interjected, smiling.

"And you hurled up every last one them on the sidewalk!" Linda laughed. "I think one landed on my boot."

Bear noticed a hint of sadness in Sophie's face.

"You must've had a good reason for drinking like that," she prompted.

Sophie took a sip from her own mug as she contemplated her answer. The café's lights were still dimmed, and the glow lay softly on her wispy, red hair.

Bear watched her profile: how she held her mug with two hands; her small chin and slightly pointed ears; her thin, sinewy frame; how she sat cross-legged on the sofa, her glittery purple toenails on display.

She's a fairy, Bear thought and smiled.

"My wife..." Sophie began, then turned her gaze to Bear. "My wife had just left me."

Wife? Bear thought. *The country won't let us get married yet, but* ... Bear recalled the afternoon in Inwood Park when she had knelt in the leaves with Nonna's ring in her hand. She winced and felt a pinch in her heart.

Sophie must have seen Bear's face. "We took a sacred vow," she said. "She *was* my wife."

Bear had often wondered what would have happened if Marabella had said yes that afternoon and if they had taken their own vows. Could Marabella have endured being an exile from her own family? Would their relationship have survived such isolation? In the end, Bear believed Marabella's rejection had saved them both from a greater pain than the heartbreak of their ending.

"Why did she leave?" Bear asked before catching herself. "I'm sorry. That was—"

"She was unfaithful," Sophie said, forcing the words up through her throat.

Bear shifted in her seat and looked at Linda, who was studying the deep interior of her mug.

"Wow, I'm sorry," Bear said. She felt suddenly awkward, presented with Sophie's sad face and Linda's avoidance. "I don't think I could ever forgive something like that... again." Her mind traveled back to her twenty-year-old self crying on the steps outside her apartment, where she had waited all night for her girlfriend to come home. "The first woman I ever fell in love with had an affair with my best friend," she said, hoping to break the awkward tension with her own pathetic story.

"Whoa!" Linda murmured, looking up from her mug. "That's brutal."

"The crazy thing is I was going to leave her. Then at the last minute I gave her a second chance. I remember it was the night before my move. All my things were packed, and for some reason I was in the bathroom scrubbing the tub. I don't know why. Maybe I didn't want to leave a trace of me behind or something. She walked into the bathroom and just watched me scrub. Finally, I stopped and looked at her, and she looked so sad. She said, 'We don't have to do this, you know.' And just like that, I gave in. I stayed."

Linda snorted. "You give in easy!"

"What happened?" Sophie asked.

Bear shrugged. "I thought I had forgiven her, but I was just fooling myself. I remember being so angry and suspicious all the time." She sighed. "In the end, I took a flamethrower to what was left of our relationship."

"Forgiveness can't be forced or faked," said Sophie.

"Would you ever forgive *her*?" asked Bear.

"One day maybe." Sophie tilted her head. "But forgiveness is a double-edged sword."

"I'll say," mumbled Linda. "Best to leave it alone."

"Why?" Bear asked Sophie, ignoring Linda.

"Forgiving frees us in a way, but it can make it harder to walk away."

"Bingo!" Linda exclaimed.

Bear looked at Linda, then back at Sophie.

"It must have taken a lot of courage to get back out there again," she said.

"It does," said Sophie. "And I haven't."

Bear's eyes widened. "Oh, um..." she stuttered. "I thought you and Linda..."

Linda looked up from her mug and laughed good-naturedly.

"Just friends, Bear Bear," she said. "I dragged her out of the house tonight."

"Literally," Sophie chuckled. "I have the marks to prove it."

"Told her it was a rescue mission."

"It was!" Bear exclaimed. They had no idea how much help they'd been to her that night.

"Was this place your idea?" Sophie asked after a moment.

"Yes," said Bear. "I wanted..." She paused, realizing she hadn't really said it out loud before. "I wanted to create a place where we all could feel free, and..."

"Like we belong," said Sophie, completing Bear's thought.

Bear nodded. "And I wanted to make food and feed people the way my nonna taught me."

"That's a beautiful vision," said Sophie. "You can feel it when you enter. You can feel her too."

Bear felt a welling-up behind her eyes. Nonna was still such a tender spot for her.

Sophie's gaze settled on Bear. "You created this place for *you*, didn't you?" she asked. "And for *her*."

Bear nodded, conscious of the lump in her throat. Somehow, Sophie saw her intentions without having to ask.

"What about Ronnie?" asked Linda. "What does she think about the café?"

"It's just a business to her," said Bear. "She wants to create a chain."

"That's a whole other vision," said Linda. Sophie nodded.

Linda topped off all three coffee mugs with more wine. Mazzy Star haunted the room with a sad song about two lovers becoming strangers and turning "Into Dust." Sophie closed her eyes and moved her head slightly to the music.

"Is Ronnie really working on franchising in San Diego?" Linda asked. She put the bottle on the coffee table and plunked herself back down on the loveseat.

Bear thought of the unanswered messages and calls on her phone in the kitchen. "I don't think so."

Linda nodded and rolled up the sleeves of her white linen shirt. She took a healthy sip of wine and tapped invisible sweat from her brow with a napkin.

"Everyone knows an addict can spot addict behavior," Linda began, "and, unfortunately, I—"

"Am an addict?" Sophie grinned saucily, her eyes still closed.

Linda tilted her face and slit her eyes toward Sophie. "Unfortunately, I am a recovering philanderer. Not proud of it."

"Philanderer?" Sophie raised a brow, then opened one eye toward Linda.

Linda ignored the question and straightened a napkin on the coffee table. "And I can smell a cheater, so let's get to the bottom of this, Bear Bear."

"How do we do that?" asked Bear.

Linda leaned forward. "Tell me everything."

An hour later, Bear checked her phone but didn't read the three missed messages from Ronnie. Instead she rummaged through the bottom of her backpack, past the bottle of Prozac, until her fingers found her emergency pack of Djarums. She reached into the back of a shelf for a bottle. Time to drink that bottle of red Micki had given her, she thought.

She had told Linda about the three Chinese letters tattooed on Ronnie's lower back.

"Oh boy." Linda shook her head. "No one gets a tramp stamp that says 'good health,' Bear Bear. Not in any language."

And Bear had told her about Isabel, the late nights, and how Ronnie had suddenly shaved her yoni clean as a baby's bottom.

"Well, do you like a shaved coochie?" Linda asked. "She could have done it for you."

Bear felt Sophie's eyes on the side of her face.

61

"No," she said, her cheeks flushing. "I like... hair."

Linda opened the second bottle and poured a generous portion into each mug. They sat in silence while Nick Drake sang "Three Hours" in an urgent and melancholic voice that hung, like cigarette smoke, in the air above them.

"The question," Linda began, with folded hands and lowered eyes, "is not what Ronnie is doing, Bear." She lifted her gaze with a faint grimace. "The question is what *you're* going to do."

"I don't know." Bear's head was swirling. It wasn't so much that Ronnie was unfaithful. This, to Bear's surprise, registered little emotion. No crushing sense of betrayal. No stabbing pain in the heart. What swirled in Bear's mind was Linda's question. What *was* she going to do? Leave Ronnie? How would she live? She had already quit her teaching job to run the café, and Les Beans didn't make enough to live on yet. She couldn't afford to move out on her own. Suddenly Bear realized how trapped she was. Everything she owned had Ronnie's name on it. Her home. The café. Then a new, more frightening thought cut Bear's breath short. What would it take to break free of Ronnie?

"Bear?" Sophie's voice pierced through the buzz of her thoughts. "Are you all right? You look like your head might explode."

"I think I need some air," Bear said, standing quickly and looking at the door, "and a smoke."

"You smoke?" asked Linda.

"Just—just these Indonesian clove things."

"Cool." Linda pulled a small ziplock bag from her side pocket. "I just smoke these Californian things."

The night outside the coffeehouse was cool for July in Florida—a benefit of being so close to the ocean—and a breeze from the east gently moved the leaves of the old mango tree above them. The three sat on a long, wooden bench under the tree, across from a small bistro table outside the kitchen door. Bear sat in the middle and could hear Sophie to her right breathing in the night air and Linda to her left flicking her lighter. Bear lit her Black and exhaled a blue cloud of clove-scented smoke into the leaves above.

"What a beautiful tree," Sophie said.

"I think that's why I picked this place," said Bear and chuckled softly at the memory of that afternoon. "I was driving by, and it caught my eye. Almost drove over the curb turning in."

"She called you, then."

"Who?"

"The tree."

Bear thought about this for a moment. It had certainly felt like a nudge.

"Maybe," she said. "I do think a spirit lives in her."

"All trees have spirits," said Sophie.

Bear glanced at Sophie, whose gaze was still lifted toward the branches above. Sophie had no idea how closely her words echoed Nonna's, or how comforting that felt to Bear.

"Some of my customers say they talk to her," she said, blowing another cloud into the branches.

"Do you?" asked Sophie, her gaze shifting from the branches above to Bear.

Bear pondered this under Sophie's gaze, which, even in the darkness, was difficult to hold. She had a sense that Sophie would be pleased if she said, *Oh, yes. I talk to the tree all the time,* but she had an even stronger sense that, even in these first new moments of their friendship she could not lie or exaggerate. The truth was, Bear wasn't conscious of communicating with the tree at all, but often felt drawn to sit beneath it, lean against it, and look at the sky through its bright green leaves. The tree felt like an ancient matriarch, protective and patient. In a strange way, this mango tree felt like Nonna herself.

This sudden realization stirred a sadness in Bear.

"I hardly talk to my nonna," she said. "She's the one I should be talking to right now."

"She passed away?" asked Linda.

"This past October." Bear sighed. She touched the ring on the chain around her neck. "She gave me this for my graduation." She took a drag from her cigarette. "She was the only one."

"The only one?" Sophie asked.

"The only one who came."

Linda lifted the ring, leaned closer, and squinted at the small, silver band with three imbedded gemstones. "It's beautiful," she said. "I knew there was a story behind this."

"What was she like?" asked Sophie.

Bear laughed as the image of Nonna in her kitchen came into view. "Magical," she said. "Sparky."

Sophie smiled and nudged Bear playfully with her shoulder.

"So do you *look* like her, too?" she asked.

Bear laughed and felt tears tickling her warm cheeks.

"I really like you guys," she murmured. Her face pinched, and she tried to swallow her sobs, but they came in shudders. She didn't know exactly why she was crying. She had felt a sudden upwelling of emotion sitting between Linda and Sophie's soft and safe shoulders, aware of Linda's protective presence and Sophie's ability to see her and understand her without words. Maybe she cried because she hadn't felt this way in so very long—since those Christmas evenings years ago, when she had curled up in the warmth of Marabella and the glow of little angels on the tree.

"Dance with me, Sophie!" Linda shouted. Back inside, she had changed the CD and turned up the volume. Dave Matthews sang "Crash into Me," and Linda twirled around on the stage alone. "You, too, Bear!"

Sophie put her mug down, hopped onto the stage, which stood only four inches above the floor, and looked back at Bear.

Bear couldn't remember the last time she had danced. Ronnie didn't care for dancing, and, outside of slow-dancing to Luis Miguel in her living room, Marabella had always feared someone from her church might see her if they danced in public.

Linda spun Sophie around, singing the lyrics to her, which Sophie didn't notice at all because she danced with her eyes closed. Bear laughed at the sight of her new friends and swayed on the floor next the stage. *Not quite dancing*, she thought, *but a start.*

"What's that?" asked Linda, turning down the volume and tilting her head toward the door.

Someone was tapping on the front window.

Linda looked at her phone.

"It's two a.m., Bear." A note of worry crept into her voice.

"Stay here, please." Bear edged toward the window. She crouched behind a plant and squinted at the figure standing just outside, peering in. The light from the sign above the figure illuminated familiar features.

Bear moved to the door.

The man gave her a toothless smile. His sallow, unshaven face was withered; his sunken cheeks cast odd shadows across his face. He wore a greasy, sleeveless shirt and loose, stained cargo shorts held up by a deflated bicycle tube.

"Hey! Wait!" called Linda.

Sophie had already slid behind Bear, her eyes fixed on the man in the window.

Bear reached for the door and unlocked the dead bolt.

"Hey, Simon!" she said. "Everything OK?"

"Everything OK with you?" Simon leaned through the open door and looked around, eying Linda and Sophie suspiciously. "I saw the lights on, and then I saw your car, and then I started thinking, 'Bear don't stay this late.'"

"Aw, Simon!" Bear exclaimed. "I'm sorry. I was just hanging out with friends."

"All right, all right." Simon waved and smiled at Sophie. "Don't want nothin' to happen to ya, is all."

"Hang on a sec, Simon." Bear grabbed a handful of something from behind the counter and returned to the door. She put a mound of Werther's into Simon's greasy palm. "I appreciate you looking out for me."

After he had gone, Sophie asked, "Where does Simon live?"

"Under the stairs," answered Bear.

"Sounds like a horror movie," grumbled Linda.

Bear laughed. "The owner of the bar across the street lets him live in the enclosed area under the stairs," she explained.

"Just be careful, Bear," Linda said.

"Simon is pretty harmless," Bear assured her.

"He has kind eyes," added Sophie.

"You could see his eyes?" asked Linda, and seemed alarmed that Sophie had gotten that close.

"I always got a kind vibe from him," Bear agreed.

"Some people believe angels walk among the homeless," Sophie added.

"I can see that." Bear nodded.

"Some people believe serial killers hide among the homeless," Linda insisted, rifling through a pile of CDs.

"You up, Bear Bear?" Linda lifted her head and squinted.

It was early morning. They had stayed in the café all night, having fallen to sleep on the sofas.

Bear stood at the front window and smiled at the eastern sky, her eyes fixed on a blooming pink cloud that looked like a laughing bear cub.

"Want to watch the sunrise?" she asked.

"I'd love to," inserted Sophie from the sofa.

"I'll bring the music," said Linda, searching the floor for her sandals.

"I've got a blanket in my car," Sophie offered.

Bear had risen earlier, when the first light of day created a blue-gray glow in the front window, and she had stood, peering to the east, listening to the occasional click and whir of the espresso machine. Sophie had slept curled like a cat at the other end of the sofa, and Linda, sprawled on the loveseat with one foot flung off the side. The sight of this, the empty bottles and coffee mugs on the coffee table, the slumbering new friends on the sofas, made Bear's heart feel light, happy, like it had just exhaled for the first time in years.

The beach was quiet except for the soft, rolling waves of low tide and the squawk of seagulls hovering above the fishermen. Plates clattered and the morning waitstaff at Benny's on the Pier bustled about, readying tables and putting up umbrellas. Sophie, Linda, and Bear sat on Sophie's colorful blanket and watched the sandpipers run along the edges of the foamy water and skitter close to their feet.

"When do you need to get back?" asked Linda.

"I open at ten today."

The orange sun peeked over the horizon, and the whole sky glowed with the soft pinks and blues of morning. Bear reached in her bag for her old Nikon and snapped a picture of the bright horizon.

Seized by a fierce impulse, she set her camera down, then waded in knee-deep, her trousers clinging to her shins. *I could swim into the new day.* She walked farther, deeper, until the cool, salty water soaked her shirt and splashed her face.

Bear dove into the smooth, welcoming ocean and swam out toward the rising sun.

Nonna, she whispered, *I need you. Are you there?*

A wave rolled toward Bear, lifting her gently, the spray catching the golden light of the morning, and Bear heard it, first a whisper close to her heart, then a murmur in the gentle fall of the wave.

Always, Little Bear.

"Rough night?" A fisherman chuckled as he passed their blanket. Sophie and Linda lay soaking in the salty beach air and the first whiff of breakfast drifting off the pier. Bear sat next to them—fully clothed, wet, and sandy—drying in the sun.

"It was wonderful, actually," Bear replied.

"What was?" Linda asked, squinting.

"Last night."

Linda chuckled. "Yep. That's what all the ladies say."

"Ahem!" Sophie cleared her throat. "So much for being a recovering—what was it you said? It had such a sophisticated sound to it. Oh yes! *Philander-er. Phil-and-er-errr.*"

Linda sighed loudly. "Remind me never to do mushrooms with you."

"I'm going to head back," Bear said finally. "I've got a couple of hours before open."

"Hey, let me know if you need anything," Linda said.

"Me too, Bear," Sophie added.

"Well," said Bear, standing at the edge of the blanket. "I may need help finding a new place to live."

Linda and Sophie sat up together and shaded their eyes from the rising sun.

"You helped me decide. I'm leaving Ronnie," she clarified.

"Good call, Bear Bear!" Linda nodded.

"You've got this," said Sophie.

"And thanks again for last night," said Bear. "I had a wonderful time."

"Hey, what can I say?" Linda grinned.

"You can say, 'Thank you. I had a wonderful time, too,'" Sophie instructed.

"Thank you," Linda echoed, playfully elbowing Sophie. "I had a wonderful time too."

Bear walked across the bridge over the canal and looked out over the glistening water. Under the bridge men and women cast their lines toward the pilings where the snook gathered to feed on snails and muscles. Soon the tide would come in, bringing ocean perch, trout, and drum. Bear looked over the rail at the waters below. The incoming tide had not yet arrived, and the water below the bridge was still. Slack tide. The in-between, when the energy gathers below the still waters on the surface, building the strength it needs for movement and momentum. Then slowly, like a train, the current rolls out again, gaining strength and speed, becoming unstoppable.

Bear sighed and walked on. If only life were that unstoppable.

Chapter 5

On Friday evening, after closing the café, Bear made the twenty-minute drive south on 95 to Boca. She entered the house timidly, like a stranger in someone else's home. A trespasser. Had this dwelling ever been hers? she wondered. She thought of the words in that Talking Heads song, "Once in a Lifetime."

She remembered working so hard at making this place feel like home when they had first bought it. She had pulled up the outdated shag carpet, painted the walls, and chipped up old tile. She had laid new sod in the front yard, then planted flowers and a cute powderpuff tree that sprinkled the yard with little pink puffs of magic. Her relationship with Ronnie had been so filled with logic and bottom lines, duties and responsibilities that there was no room left for magic, so Bear carved out little places

Patricia Lucia

in the yard that felt magical to her and placed stumps there to sit.

Ronnie had reasoned that because Bear's school schedule allowed her to arrive home earlier she could use that time to prepare the evening meals and tidy the house. Bear would have found joy in meal preparation if Ronnie had any appreciation at all for the sensuous nature of spices and the healing and mystical qualities of herbs. Ronnie's logical mind—made solely of straight lines and sharp angles—afforded no room for such notions nor deference for any meal said to be *cooked with love*, and her taste buds obeyed.

"There are only two spices you need when preparing food for me," Ronnie would say, usually after tasting a dish made with cumin or coriander or Bear's favorite herb, rosemary. "Salt and pepper."

"Salt isn't a spice," Bear usually corrected her.

Ronnie began calling ahead on her way home.

"What's for dinner?" She'd ask, and if she suspected Bear had added an unwanted spice or herb to dinner, would say, "OK, I'll stop and get a rotisserie at Publix."

Bear walked into the master bedroom and put her backpack down. She would move her things into the guest room before Ronnie returned, she decided. She wasn't going to sleep in this bed again.

76

She sat on the edge of it—just one more time—and lay back, exhausted. Little specks of glitter in the popcorn ceiling twinkled in the soft lamplight. She had loved to look at the twinkling ceiling in the early morning light when she first woke. It had brought comfort and distraction when she lay sleepless and alone on more recent nights. She remembered getting lost in the blurring, glittery twinkles when Ronnie made love to her, but that seemed like such a long time ago.

She had just started to doze when the doorbell rang, and so she got up and trudged barefoot to the entryway. Jack, their neighbor, peered through the front window. He wasn't one to knock, especially not when Ronnie was away.

Bear didn't care for Jack. He wasn't fond of her either.

"Hey, Jack," Bear said as she opened the door. "What's up?"

"I'm just checking on you," he said. "Ronnie called and was worried because you weren't answering your phone."

"Oh yeah," Bear said. "It died. I'm charging it now."

"Huh," Jack said with a half nod, like a detective scanning a suspect. "I didn't see your car here last night either, so that got her even more worried, as

Patricia Lucia

you can imagine. That café isn't in the best neighborhood."

"Yeah, it was a late night," Bear replied. "I crashed at the café."

Jack chuckled, but there was nothing good-natured about it. "Yeah, well, looks like it was one helluva party," he said, eying her rumpled trousers as he turned to walk away. "Better call her, though," he yelled over his shoulder.

Shit. Bear grabbed her backpack, pulled out her dead phone, and plugged it in by the nightstand in the guest room. She didn't want to let on to Ronnie that she was leaving her. Not yet. Not until she had an idea of where the hell she was going.

She reached into the bottom of her bag for her cloves and absently grabbed the camera. Picking grains of sand off its hardware seemed like a perfect distraction from thinking about the conversation she would eventually have to have with Ronnie.

Bear went outside, sat on the swing, and lit a clove cigarette. She held the camera close to inspect it for sand, but squinted instead at an unfamiliar picture on the viewfinder: a golden sun over a smooth ocean; a dark figure floating on the surface of the glimmering, orange-and-pink water. Someone had taken that picture. They must have known she would need to remember the morning she had

78

swum into the sunrise, would need to carry it like a talisman. Bear smiled. She knew exactly who had taken it.

Bear woke early Saturday morning feeling rested and peaceful despite her exchange with their nosy neighbor, Jack, and her avoidance of Ronnie's calls the day before. She sipped her second cup of coffee and scrolled through all her unread messages.

Ronnie's texts had grown longer and angrier overnight. They began to feel like hounds, nipping and snarling at Bear's heels. She poured most of her second cup into the sink and noticed a slight tremble in her fingers. The prickly feeling in the back of her neck had returned. *So much for peace*, she thought.

She had not expected Ronnie's reaction. Rather, she had imagined Ronnie would disappear into the San Diego sunset with Isabel, then reappear again, if she did at all, on Sunday night or Monday or whenever she planned to return. Ronnie hadn't said a word about her itinerary, where she was staying, her flights, her plans. Nothing. And where was Isabel? For someone who had just concocted an excuse to spend a weekend with her other girlfriend, as Bear suspected Isabel to be, Ronnie was spending a lot of time on the phone. Maybe she was wrong about Isabel, Bear thought. After all, she was straight, according to Ronnie. Then again, so was Marabella.

Bear read the last message sent at four in the morning and winced as she read Ronnie's dissertation on the ways Bear had taken advantage of her generosity, had used her to have a better life, a much better life than anything she had had in New York. Bear had used her money—*our money*, Bear corrected—to open a lesbian coffee joint so she could have plenty of women around. *You've offered no explanation*, it continued, *for why you haven't returned my calls and why you never came home on Thursday.*

Bear let out a long sigh. The more hours that passed and the angrier Ronnie got, the more Bear wanted to avoid speaking to her altogether. The thought of defending herself against Ronnie's tsunami of accusations already felt exhausting, and worse, the thought of telling Ronnie she was leaving her was downright terrifying.

She opened the folding doors of the master bedroom closet and pulled out a pair of pants, then another. Soon a heap of her clothes lay on the bed, and the purge turned to the dresser, creating a second pile of underwear, socks, and T-shirts. She cleared the odds and ends from the nightstand on her side, then stood in the center of the room looking at the piles on the bed, calculating the number of boxes it would take to pack up her life.

She had just moved her toiletries to the guest bathroom, put her toothbrush in a cup by the sink, and collected her shampoo from the master bathroom's en suite shower when the doorbell rang. Bear sighed and pulled her bathrobe tight around her waist.

"Hello again, Jack," she said, opening the inside door and speaking through the screen.

Jack stood with a phone to his ear and eyed Bear.

"Yeah," he said, "she's here." He held the phone toward the screen. "Ronnie wants to speak to you."

Bear shoved her hands in her bathrobe pockets.

"If she wants to speak to me, she can call me," she said. "On my phone." Bear could hear Ronnie's voice from where she stood.

"She says your phone doesn't seem to be working," Jack said and held the phone toward the screen again.

Bear opened the door, took the phone, and closed the screen.

"Do you want me to wait out here?" Jack asked.

Bear raised the phone to her ear. "For god's sakes, Adelina. You have his phone. Let him in!" Ronnie spouted.

Ignoring her own feelings, Bear opened the door to the narc.

"What the hell is going on?" Ronnie yelled.

"With what?" Bear asked, holding her voice steady.

"Don't play stupid," Ronnie steamed. "I know you didn't come home on Thursday."

"Neither did you."

"So that's your excuse?"

Bear eyed Jack edging his way down the hall toward the open door of the bedroom.

"Ronnie, you have no idea how hard it is to run that place alone on a Thursday night," she said as calmly as she could muster.

"What the hell does that have to do with anything?"

"I worked my ass off Thursday," Bear said. "It took forever to clean up. So I crashed there, OK? So what?"

"Alone?"

"Yes, alone," Bear lied, pressing her lips firmly together.

"You could have told me that Thursday night." Ronnie's anger had just come down a notch.

Bear wanted to ask her why she had needed to leave in such a rush in the first place, but she knew better.

"Are you feeling prepared for today?"

"For what?" Ronnie said. She sounded distracted or stressed, Bear couldn't tell which. Ronnie didn't seem to be thinking about the presentation at all.

Maybe there is no presentation, Bear thought. She took a breath. She wanted her voice to sound as neutral as possible.

"The presentation."

"I'd feel more prepared if I hadn't been trying to get hold of you for the last two days."

Bear watched Jack stop in front of the master bedroom and look at the piles of Bear's clothes on the bed.

"Where's Isabel?" Bear asked with feigned concern. "Hasn't she been helping out?"

"She couldn't fly in until this morning." Ronnie sounded genuinely upset. This time, not with Bear. "Things came up." The phone went silent except for a muffled, rhythmic sound that after a few moments Bear recognized as an iron moving in jerky motions, releasing steam. Bear remembered Ronnie's persistent texts on Thursday night after having left so early and without regard for the fact she'd made Bear handle the open mic night crowd alone. And the angry, accusing texts the next day. Maybe Ronnie had been more upset with Isabel than with her. And maybe the *Where the hell are you?* and *Why aren't you answering?* messages were meant for Isabel too.

"Well, I've got to get to the café," Bear said. "Good luck today."

"What?" Ronnie said faintly. "Oh, yeah. Sure. I'll be fine."

Bear handed the phone back to Jack, who gazed at her with an odd smirk. He stepped out of the front door and put the phone to his ear.

"It looks kinda weird in there," he said, and then his voice moved out of range.

Chapter 6

Bear woke to the whining, churning sound of a lawn edger revving, then idling, then revving again. The sound pierced the whole house, polluting every bubble of peace and quiet, even the guest room in the back, where Bear lay with a pillow pressed over her ears.

She got up, scuffled sleepily to the living room window, and peered through the shutters toward the noise. Of course Jack had decided to manicure his lawn at seven on a Sunday morning.

She checked her phone and was surprised at first to see no messages, then remembered Isabel had arrived in San Diego yesterday morning. Bear was surprised that she felt a sense of relief with this. Still, how odd, she thought, to feel so little.

Her thoughts returned to Marabella and the last months of their relationship. They had agreed to end it just after that sad Christmas, but neither knew how to let go. Marabella suggested Bear start dating, so Bear had reluctantly gone speed dating in the village. The memory of her first date rushed back to her now. She had gotten drunk and called Marabella from the bar, making some incomprehensible argument for why Marabella should marry her after all. Why Marabella should leave her family and come away with her. *I can be your family*, she had cried pitifully. *I can make you happy*. Bear closed her eyes to the memory. Such a desperate and hopeless love, a wound that still pinched her heart, as if a ghost lingered there, haunting a secret chamber.

Bear was not in love with Ronnie—she had put aside such desires long ago—and though this spared her the painful price she had paid with Marabella, she wondered what the cost might be when she ended things with Ronnie.

For now, she had boxes to pack. She wanted to do it in peace, and she wanted Jack to stay on his side of the street. She would rather listen to that damn lawn edger all morning than hear his knock at the door.

Bear had just finished her first cup of coffee when her phone rang with a message. She was surprised to see it was Sophie.

I know it's a little early... but would you like to come see a miracle?

A wave of excitement rippled through her to her fingers as she replied. *It's never too early for miracles.*

You'll have to hurry. Come to Lake Worth Beach just south of the pier.

On my way!

Bear threw on a pair of shorts and a T-shirt and grabbed her keys. Jack managed to step in front of her car as she pulled out of the driveway.

"Where you off to in such a hurry?" he asked over the idling lawn edger.

"Church!" Bear exclaimed, and smiled into her rearview mirror at his contorted face.

The morning breeze carried tiny droplets of ocean water across the boardwalk and up the stairs by the lifeguard station, where Bear stepped onto the cool sand of the beach. Farther down, a group had gathered in an excited circle. She saw Sophie step outside the circle and wave at her.

"What's happening?" Bear asked, imagining that some strange sea creature had washed ashore.

"I told you," said Sophie. "A miracle."

Sophie took Bear's hand and led her through the circle of people who had gathered: fishermen with long, scraggly, white beards; surfers with wild, sun-bleached hair; women wearing tie-dye T-shirts; and a child in a sandy-bottomed bathing suit. All of them looked intently at a hole in the sand. Bear leaned in and noticed the hole itself was moving and the sand shifting.

"Baby sea turtles!" Sophie whispered. "Have you ever seen them hatch?"

"Never," Bear said, mesmerized by the movement. A little black snout appeared in one place, a little flipper in another. She looked toward the water, about fifty feet away. The waves were breaking farther out, but still clapped the shore with a low rumble and stretched their reach onto the sand. The tide was coming in.

The tiny turtles emerged—first one, then two, then a small wave. The onlookers used their hands to clear a path in the sand for the babies, and soon a stream of moving life edged its way in little flecks toward the water. Bear felt Sophie watching her and realized her mouth was open and her eyes were wide in wonder.

"Which one is you?" Sophie asked.

Bear laughed. "That one." She pointed to a baby turtle making its way up the side of the mound of sand.

"That's me," Sophie said, giggling, and pointed to a baby wandering off the cleared path. "Let's race to the water."

Bear laughed. "Well, your little Sophie is moving in the wrong direction."

"Don't underestimate her!" Sophie warned. "C'mon, Baby Sophie!"

Bear watched her baby turtle move in jerking motions toward the water, its tiny flippers awkward and unsteady like a baby's first steps. "C'mon, Baby Bear!"

Some of the hatchlings had reached the water's edge and disappeared into the foamy waves. Some were carried back onto the beach again and again while others were carried out into the churning water.

When Bear's baby turtle reached the water, she shouted, "My baby won! Baby Bear won!"

"Well," said Sophie, "little Sophie let you win."

"Really?" Bear said, tilting her head incredulously. "How does that work, exactly?"

"Simple," Sophie said without hesitation. "Baby Sophie says, 'After you, little sister. You can go first.'"

"Oh, really?" Bear chuckled.

"Absolutely," Sophie said. "In baby turtle language."

Bear laughed. "If they're all part of the same nest, aren't they technically twins?"

Sophie smiled and surrendered. "Yes, they are."

Most of the turtles had made their way to the water, speckling the low, turquoise waves with moving, black polka dots. The people who had gathered and cleared the way now stood and watched the babies disappear into the surf. So small, so new, swimming into such a vast ocean without any sense at all of their own courage, thought Bear. They were pulled by some ancient memory like an invisible current.

"So perilous," Bear murmured.

"Yes," said Sophie.

"And yet," Bear said, her voice filled with wonder, "it's so beautiful."

"That's the miracle," Sophie replied, transfixed on a point in the distant horizon.

The café felt, as it did on most Sundays, like a warm and intimate living room. Bear opened at noon, and her regulars trickled in from the beach, still sandy and barefoot and looking like they had just made love.

As the day slowed in the late afternoon, Bear retreated to the kitchen and the last pile of dishes in the sink. With her hands in the warm, soapy water, she daydreamed about the baby turtles' wobbly march into their life in the ocean and the way Sophie's hand had felt in hers. She wondered what Sophie had seen on the horizon. Bear's reverie was interrupted by the ringing of her phone.

"I've got some great news, Bear Bear!" Linda exclaimed. "I think I found you a place!"

"What?" Bear blurted.

"Now this is a little unusual," Linda began. "This friend of mine, a Realtor, has a house for sale on Lakeside. Furnished and staged for selling, but the place has been on the market for months, and who knows when it will sell? He's looking for someone to stay there, keep things clean and tidy for any possible showings. He'll rent it to you for almost nothing. He'd like to help you out too."

"So..." Bear's mind spun. "The house is for sale..."

"Yeah, but you could probably live there for months before they get a serious offer."

Bear's heart began to race. "Did he say how much?"

"Five hundred a month!" exclaimed Linda. "Can you believe that? You could cover that with tips!"

"When is it available?" Bear said. She felt as if she had just inhaled helium and might squeak or float or pop.

"Right now."

On Monday morning, Bear pulled up to the curb in front of a two-story Spanish-style house on Lakeside Avenue and checked her messages before getting out of the car. Ronnie had been on radio silence since Saturday, and Bear had no idea when she was coming home. If this place was everything Linda had said it was—available now and at a price she could afford—she would have to have the dreaded conversation with Ronnie sooner than she thought.

Linda waved to her from the front step, and Bear chuckled at the contrast between Linda's strong, no-nonsense presence, her tall stature and swagger, and the colorful scrubs she wore to work. Today she wore teal scrubs with cartoon dinosaurs and bright blue Crocs. The only thing that said no-nonsense in her appearance was the tight ponytail that held back her long, sandy brown hair.

"Dinosaurs today?" Bear said with a wink.

"The kids love them."

"It's pink!" Bear commented on the house's exterior as Linda opened the front door.

"Don't let that fool you," Linda said, opening the heavy wooden door. "This house is badass!"

Bear entered the foyer and looked to the right, toward the living room where a mahogany grand piano sat in the corner. A plump sofa faced a fireplace, and a small table with two chairs nestled under a picture window framed by stained glass hummingbirds in flight.

"Holy shit," murmured Bear.

"Check out the kitchen!" Linda's voice pealed from down the hall.

Bear gazed in amazement at the maple cabinets, black granite countertops, and stainless steel appliances. *How could this be nicer than my Boca house?* she thought.

"I know it may feel fast," said Linda after they had walked through all the rooms, "but the first of the month is on Thursday. You can move in then if you want to make it happen."

She could make this happen, Bear thought. She could picture it. Reading peacefully on the sofa. Drinking morning coffee in the chair by the window. Watching the early morning light illuminate the stained glass hummingbirds.

Then Bear felt her stomach drop and the edges of dread seep in. First, she had to face Ronnie.

Sometime after midnight that night, Bear heard the garage door open. She sat up in bed, startled, disoriented, and a little frightened. A moment later she realized Ronnie had arrived home. Her breath quickened and her heart thumped against her chest. She crept to the door of the guest room and turned the lock. Ronnie would have to keep her anger on the other side if it came to that. Bear wondered how strong the bedroom door really was. It wasn't solid wood like the doors in her old New York apartment. This door was decorative on the outside and hollow on the inside. If Ronnie really wanted to get in, it wouldn't take much.

Ronnie's suitcase rolled across the floor into the master bedroom; then there was silence. Bear waited, listening, her heart beating loudly in her chest.

"Adelina?" Ronnie's voice sounded like that of a parent who has just discovered their child's messy room. Footsteps approached the door, and Bear, in her panic, contemplated hiding under the bed.

"Adelina?" A soft knock rattled the door. The doorknob moved, then jiggled. "Adelina, are you in there?"

Bear froze, her hands covering her mouth with a corner of the blanket.

"Adelina!" Ronnie yelled.

"Yes...?" she finally relented.

"What are you doing in there?"

"I wanted to sleep in here."

"What the hell for?"

"Because I don't want to sleep... with you," she said, just loud enough for Ronnie to hear through the door. Then she added more softly, "Anymore."

"Are you kidding me right now, Adelina?" The volume of Ronnie's voice rose with each word.

"No."

"Are you alone in there?" Ronnie yelled, pulling on the knob and pounding the door with her fist. "Open this fucking door!"

"Yes, I am alone!" Bear shouted above Ronnie. "And—and I want to go to sleep." Her voice cracked. "I want to be alone!"

"I don't have time for your craziness right now, Adelina," Ronnie said, exasperated. "Stay in there if you want to, but sooner or later, you have to come out." When Bear didn't respond, she added, "You can't stay in there forever."

Ronnie's footsteps moved across the tile floor to the master bedroom, and the door slammed. Bear barely slept a wink the rest of the night. She finally drifted off in the morning when the garage door opened again and Ronnie's car pulled out of the driveway.

When Bear's phone rang for the first time that day, the midmorning sun shone brightly through the guest bedroom window. Bear let it ring. A moment later it rang again, and Bear squinted at the screen. Ronnie's face smiled up at her, taunting her.

"I can't do this right now, Ronnie," she mumbled. But the phone rang a third time, and, defeated, Bear reached toward the sound.

"Where are your things?" demanded Ronnie.

"In boxes in the spare room."

"What the hell for?" Though she'd used those words before, Ronnie's tone of voice cut into her.

"Because I'm leaving."

"Because you're *what?*"

"I'm leaving," Bear said as resolutely as she could.

Ronnie let out a loud, cynical laugh.

"Where are you going, Adelina?" The question felt just as biting as her laughter.

"I'm moving out."

Ronnie let out another dry laugh. "You're moving out," she repeated.

"Yes." Bear wanted to say as few words as possible to hide the tremble in her voice.

Ronnie was silent. Wind blew against the receiver. She must have stepped outside the hospital to make the call.

"Are you moving in with someone?"

"No," Bear said and steadied her voice. "I found a place."

"You found a place," Ronnie repeated. "Just like that."

"Yes."

Again, the line filled with mocking laughter.

"So now that you've shared your little fantasy," Ronnie said with controlled anger, as if she spoke through gritted teeth, "let me share some reality with you. You have no money, last I checked, and you don't make enough to live on from the café, which, by the way, is half mine. Unless you're going to shack up with someone or rent a room in a ghetto, you can't afford to live on your own." Ronnie's voice had steadily risen as she spoke. "I'm just breaking it down for you, Cinderella," she concluded.

Bear was quiet for a moment. She had no counterpoint. There was no point in arguing that this was a sound and rational decision. It wasn't sound or rational, and Bear knew it.

"I know it's going to be really hard," she admitted, "but I have to do this."

"This is crazy, Adelina," Ronnie insisted. "Are you taking your medication?"

Bear was silent. No use in telling her the truth. No use lying either.

"Are you?" Ronnie pressed.

"I'm taking my life back," Bear said finally.

"Exactly what life is that, Adelina?" Ronnie shouted. "What life, huh? You *had* no life. The life you had living in that shithole apartment in Washington Heights? The life where everything you owned came from a thrift shop? That life? This is the best life you've ever had, Adelina! The best life you ever—"

Bear hung up. Whatever life she was getting herself into, rational or not, she knew it would never sound like this again.

On Wednesday evening Bear sat quietly on the edge of the bed in the guest room. She had put the last of the boxes in her car, ready for the move tomorrow, after closing the café. Linda would drop the key off in the afternoon. Exhausted, she slipped into a pair of shorts and a T-shirt and slid under the covers. Ronnie was not home yet, and the house felt peaceful. She needed a good night's sleep.

Just as Bear drifted into sleep, the garage door rumbled open and Ronnie's car idled in the garage.

A few minutes later, Ronnie knocked on the guest room door.

"Adelina?" Her voice was unsteady. "Can we talk?"

Bear got up from the bed and opened the door, then returned to sit on the edge of it with folded arms.

Ronnie looked like shit as she hovered in the doorway. Her eyes were red and puffy. She had none of her previous arrogance or anger.

"I got a little carried away yesterday," she said. "I'm sorry."

"OK," Bear said tentatively.

"I know you want to leave, and I can't stop you," Ronnie said. She looked genuinely sad. "Listen, the Pride Gala is tomorrow, and I was hoping you might want to come with me. For old times' sake."

"Why would I do that?" Bear asked.

"Because it's good for the café," Ronnie replied. Her voice was softer now, disarming.

"Tomorrow is the busiest night of the week, Ronnie," Bear said. "I really don't think—"

"I already have the tickets," Ronnie interrupted, "if you change your mind." She stepped closer, the scent of whisky mingling with her cologne.

"Think about it, Adelina," she said, her voice barely above a murmur. "One last dance." She pushed a strand of Bear's hair from her face, her hand lingering by Bear's cheek.

Bear closed her eyes and exhaled. When Ronnie was not angry or arrogant, she exuded a strength and sensuality that was hard to resist. Especially when she stood so close.

"I have to finish packing," Bear said finally, and pulled back from Ronnie's hand.

Linda and Micki worked around the room, wiping tables, picking up empty mugs, and straightening the chairs. Ben Harper sang "Please Me Like You Want To" in a gravelly voice. Micki pretended to sing the chorus to Linda, using her broomstick as a microphone, and Linda pretended to ignore her.

"That's what you should say to Ronnie if you ever see her again, Bear," Linda said across the room.

"What's that?" Bear said from the counter. She had been concentrating on counting the drawer.

"That leaving you is the best thing she could do," Linda said above the music.

Bear raised her brow and paused her counting.

"It's little late for that," she said. She thought about the boxes in the back of her Tracer and the key to her new place in her pocket. Ronnie could do what she wanted. The tide of Bear's life had turned.

The bell on the front door rang softly, startling Bear. The front door was usually locked at the end of the night. Bear caught her breath and tried to adjust her focus. Ronnie, dressed in a white tux, her bow tie undone and hanging loosely around her neck, approached the counter with one hand in her pocket and the other holding a long-stemmed rose.

"Shit," whispered Linda toward Micki, who stood frozen, her broom poised awkwardly in mid-sweep. "Speaking of Ms. Prada..."

"Dude!" Micki whispered. "Ronnie's lookin' fine as fuck!"

"I think that's the point."

"Yes, please," Micki said, leaning toward the counter on her broom and finger-waving when Ronnie glanced in her direction.

Linda groaned. Micki obviously didn't know what she knew about Ronnie. "That woman would squash you like a bug," she whispered.

Micki, still oblivious to all Ronnie's lethal edges, added, "She could squash the fuck out of me."

"What are you doing here, Ronnie?" Bear demanded.

"I've come to ask you to reconsider." Ronnie's grin had a swagger that confused Bear, until she caught the smell of whisky in the air between them.

"Why would I do that?"

"Because I love you." Ronnie's breath was again a cloud of whisky. She leaned over the counter and covered Bear's hand with hers.

Bear moved her hand away. "You're drunk, Ronnie."

That didn't seem to matter to Ronnie. "We don't have to do this, Bear."

The nickname silenced her. Stunned her. She searched for the shift in Ronnie's face, a hint of acquiescence.

Ronnie had never called her by the name Nonna had given her. It was always Adelina. From the first conversation after meeting on that Elite Singles site to introducing Bear to her family, Ronnie had insisted on Adelina. *They'll all think you're crazy,* she had said. *And they'll think I'm crazy to date a woman who insists on being called Bear.*

"Look," said Ronnie, leaning closer. "I fucked up. I admit it. I want to make it right with you, Bear."

There it was again, Bear thought.

"So I'm going to pay it forward," Ronnie said, reaching into her pocket and pulling out a small box. She placed it on the counter and slid it toward her ex. "I'm going to earn you back, Bear."

Bear stared at the little box and swallowed.

"Weren't you at the gala tonight?" she asked.

"Yes," Ronnie said. "I waited for you. Kept your ticket in my pocket thinking you might change your mind."

"Couldn't find anyone else for that ticket?" Bear asked sardonically.

"Didn't want to."

Bear shook her head and looked at the tiny, un-opened box.

"Come back home, Bear," Ronnie whispered. "Please."

Bear was stunned. She watched Ronnie's long shadow move onto the sidewalk and out of view, then snatched the box from the counter and disappeared into the kitchen. Linda and Micki scurried in behind her.

"Let's see it!" Linda said. Bear had already put it on the shelf above her prep table, between the curry powder and the sea salt. Micki looked around for something to do and pulled up the trash bag from the barrel behind Bear, though she kept her eye on the shelf. Linda removed the little box, placed it on the prep table, and opened it slowly. A radiant row of diamonds sparkled on a white gold band. Bear caught her breath.

"She really pulled out the big guns tonight, huh?"

Micki snorted over the crunch of the trash bag, and Linda sent her an eyeful of daggers. Bear stared at the glittering stones, hypnotized by the dazzling facets of white and blue.

"I don't understand what she's trying to do," Bear mumbled.

"She wants to rewrite the story, Bear Bear." Linda put her hand on Bear's shoulder. "She wants to play the prince in a Cinderella story."

Bear sighed. She did feel like a sad and sooty Cinderella, cast out in the world again with her life in a few boxes in the back of her car, a nearly homeless misfit. She didn't belong in Ronnie's world. She could never be a Boca Babe no matter how much she 'cleaned up.' And she had no magical fairies to change any of that. Maybe Ronnie just wanted her servant back, her sooty little Cinderella, the woman she could keep in check with a few well-timed and pointed questions.

"Just remember," Linda was saying softly. "In order for that story to work, the slipper has to fit."

Bear nodded.

Micki had dragged the trash out the back door and returned. She stood in the doorway and jammed her hands in her pockets. It had started to rain, and the coming storm made a light patter on the leaves of mango tree behind her.

Linda wrapped her arms around Bear and held her tightly.

"You've got this, Bear," she said gently. "You want me to follow you home and help with those boxes?"

"No." Bear sniffed. "Thanks. I'll unpack the car in the morning."

"All right then," Linda exclaimed and tussled Bear's hair. "Let's go home!" She grabbed the rose off the front counter and extended it to Micki.

"Aw, thanks!" Micki chimed. "Is this from you or Ms. Prada?"

"Shut up." Linda laughed and leaned into the kitchen again. "You good, Bear?"

"Yeah, go ahead," she said. "I'm just going to lock up, and I'll be out of here."

The two walked through the quiet coffeehouse toward the front door.

"Say, would you be interested in a worm bin for your kitchen?" Micki asked, slipping her arm in Linda's.

"No," said Linda, giving Micki a side glance.

"I could give you a deep discount." Micki pulled on Linda's arm with a grin. "I could even come over and install it."

"Yes and no." Linda chuckled.

"What?"

Linda opened the door for Micki and waited for her to pass. "Yes to coming over," she said. "No to the worms."

Micki's laughter echoed across the parking lot. "I can work with that."

Bear sat at the light on Sixth Avenue and stared ahead, her windshield wipers squeaking across the glass. She watched the red, rippling pools of water on the street and the raindrops illuminated by her headlights falling in front of her car. Just a quick left here to Lakeside and four blocks down, she thought. She felt for the key in her pocket and found the ring box instead. She'd return the damn thing tomorrow, she thought. For now she sat four blocks from a new life. A new beginning.

When the pools of light on the street ahead turned green, Bear sat for a moment, lost in the sound of the rain and its glitter under the streetlights. Somewhere above the tapping of the rain on her roof, she could hear Nonna chopping vegetables in a distant kitchen. *Thank you, Nonna*, she whispered.

She looked west toward the highway sign that read "95 South to Boca Raton," then squeezed the steering wheel and resisted the temptation to give in and go back to the familiar, the known. Taking a deep breath, as if plunging into an ocean wave, Bear turned left toward Lakeside and toward a new and unknown future.

In the Chevron station on the corner, a BMW idled with its lights off by the air dispenser. When the light turned green, its engine started and the headlights flicked on. Obscured by rain and darkness, the car moved slowly out of the station and followed at a safe distance behind Bear's car.

Chapter 7

The dream was odd. Bear woke but kept her eyes closed so she could trace the scenes before they faded. In the first scene, Linda had bent over a steel train track under the mango tree and rubbed the metal to a shine. Nonna stood as if inspecting her work, then pointed down.

"You missed a spot," she said.

Bear knew Nonna well enough to know that, even in dreams, she was a smart-ass. Linda didn't seem to get the humor, and so she rubbed harder. Then Bear dropped into another scene, where she stood on a dirt path. Nonna walked ahead of her, then stopped.

"Are you coming?" she asked.

As quickly as Bear had dropped onto the path, she was suddenly weightless and flying at great speed over an ocean, just above the glistening waves. She had awakened from this scene with the dizzying sense of being in flight.

"Yes, Nonna," she whispered as she rose from the small, soft bed in the bedroom just above the hummingbird window. "I wouldn't mind if you told me where we were going, though."

Bear stood at the counter in her new kitchen and listened to the gurgle and hiss of the coffee maker. The small, black ring box sat on the other end of the counter next to her keys, and she thumped her fingers in its direction. The drumming of her fingers grew louder and faster as a sense of urgency bloomed in her gut and radiated out into her limbs and fingers. Why had Ronnie gotten her another ridiculous ring? It was as if she didn't know Bear any better now than she had in those early, awkward months on Seaman Avenue, when she had gotten the first ridiculous ring, three diamonds set on a platinum band. Bear wore only silver. Never gold or platinum. And she liked gemstones like the turquoise, lapis, and carnelian in Nonna's ring. Never diamonds.

She needed to give this thing back.

Bear poured her coffee, and as it trickled into the cup, she heard Nonna.

Not yours.

"On this we agree, Nonna." She took a sip of coffee and moved into the living room, settling under the hummingbird window. She breathed deeply and watched the shafts of morning light cut through the pink, billowing clouds in the east.

Not yours. Nonna's words came again, as if carried on the light that illuminated the glass hummingbirds above her.

"I know, I know," Bear agreed. "It's totally ridiculous."

Bear had imagined her first morning in her new home to be more peaceful than this, but she was instead filled with a sudden intense and insistent impulse to get rid of the ring, get it out of the house and far away, as if it were a tiny grenade whose pin had been pulled.

Minutes later, she stood in the driveway, eying the boxes in her car left there because of the rain. Despite her plan to empty the car this morning, the strong urge to get to Boca nudged at her back. Bear tossed the ring box on the passenger seat and headed south.

Fresh, wet tire marks through the puddles in the Boca driveway assured Bear that Ronnie had already left for work. Bear had planned her quick drop-off on the ride down. She would put the damn thing on the kitchen counter with a note, she thought, and she contemplated the note's register. Formal perhaps, like "I cannot accept this offer." Or curt with a hint of cruelty, like "You should know better than to offer me another ridiculous ring. No, thank you. Again." Or the moral high ground: "I wish you all the best."

Inside Ronnie's house, she placed the ring box on the counter and looked round the kitchen. A single cup and spoon lay in the sink, and a hint of Ronnie's cologne hung in the air. Anxious to write the note she had rehearsed on the drive, Bear opened the small drawer where Ronnie kept her stationery and pens, but the corner of a card that lay at the top of the overstuffed drawer caught, tearing off a portion of its glittery cover.

Bear cussed under her breath. She had just damaged a card that had been sent to Ronnie. But, now that she thought of it, why would Ronnie stuff such a nice card in a drawer? The card's cover featured two linked wedding bands under the word *Congratulations!*

Bear frowned. *A little premature*, she thought. *And presumptuous, whoever you are.* She opened the torn card and read the words slowly at first, then with such growing disbelief, she had to read them over and over.

Dear Ronnie,

Thank you for the pleasure of serving you. I hope your special weekend was full of magic and romance, and I wish you and Isabel the very best. Congratulations to you both! If Isabel needs the ring resized, please send her by and I'll be happy to take care of that for you.

All the best wishes,
Lizzette Ramos
Rinaldo Jewelers, Boca Raton

Bear's thoughts spun backward. The texts, the phone calls, Ronnie showing up at the café. She grabbed the ring box, pulled out the ring, and slid it onto her ring finger. It stopped at the knuckle. Bear stood still while her thoughts zigzagged. *She said no*, thought Bear. *Isabel said no.*

Suddenly she felt dirty with the kind of soot she couldn't scrub off in a shower if she tried.

With trembling fingers she placed the ring back in the box and reached in the drawer for pen and paper. Her breath heaved as her hand moved across the page. Bear placed her note between the box and the torn card; then she removed her house key from a ring and placed it on the note.

"Goodbye, Ronnie," she said and took out her phone.

Are you sure you want to block this caller? the screen prompted. Bear hit a button and tucked her phone back into her pocket.

"Yes," she said. "I'm sure."

She slid into the driver's seat, looked in her rearview mirror, and groaned. Jack stood behind the car, barefoot, wearing cargo shorts and a shirt splashed with large, colorful parrots. He grinned over the rim of a New England Patriots mug.

"Mighty big of her to let you back in," he shouted over the car's engine. "She's a bigger man than me."

Bear swerved the car around him.

"Oops," he spouted as she maneuvered past. "Guess I was wrong."

The Tracer rolled out of the driveway and pointed north, and she pictured Ronnie arriving home later and reading her note. By then, she thought, she would be gone. Unreachable. Unfindable.

Sorry Isabel said no.
So do I.
(I don't wear glass slippers)

Later, after Bear had sat a while under the mango tree with a cup of coffee and smoked several clove cigarettes, a calm returned to her. She recalled Nonna's words. Not yours.

A text chime on her phone interrupted her thoughts.

How is your heart on this beautiful new morning? Sophie had such a strange and delightful way of communicating, Bear thought as she put her phone back in her pocket. She wasn't ready to answer that question—yet.

In the café's quiet kitchen, Bear chopped onion and garlic and cubed a large butternut squash for the day's soup, butternut squash bisque. She let her breathing slow and her sense of time fade, and she felt Nonna beside her, watching over her shoulder. Cooking with Nonna this morning was the most comforting thing she could do.

The image of Nonna's old kitchen returned to her. In her memory, Bear was three and stood on a little stool at the counter to make her first gnocchi. Nonna bent over her, rubbed flour on her little hands, and showed her how to roll the dough in her palms.

"When you make food for the people you love, Little Bear," Nonna would say, "it is important that

115

you think about how much you love them. They will feel your love when they eat it." Nonna always followed with a warning. "Never make food when you are angry," she said. "Anger makes food bitter."

After the soup was finished, Bear sat at the table outside the kitchen door, another clove cigarette lit in one hand and her phone opened to Sophie's text in the other. She took a long drag off her smoke and put it down. She wanted to answer Sophie before she opened the doors but still had no idea what to say. Her phone chimed with another message.

Are you OK? Sophie asked. Bear heaved sigh.

I will be, she answered and returned to the kitchen.

An hour later, as Bear made lunches at the griddle, she heard a husky woman's voice outside the screen door.

"Hey, do you mind if I park under your tree?"

Bear put her spatula down and peered through the screen door toward the parking lot. A tall, slim, twenty-something woman stood by her van under the mango tree, her long hair worn half loose and half in locs, with feathers and beads braided into it. She wore a tank top, had darkly tanned arms, and was barefoot under her faded overalls. Bear looked past the young woman to the van parked in the spot directly under the mango tree. She could tell from a glance that this van was the woman's home.

"Hi," Bear said. "I don't own that tree, actually."

The woman let out a laugh. "I know, right?" she said. "I was just being polite because people get... touchy about that stuff." She laughed again, a more nervous laugh this time.

Bear smiled. "You can park there as long as you'd like."

"Aw, man," exclaimed the woman, "that's awesome! I'm here for the... um... for Ali Stein." She laughed again. "I'm early."

Ali Stein, a local musician with a big following in the women's bars around South Florida, was scheduled to perform for the first time at Les Beans Café that evening. But that was in ten hours.

"You want something to drink... um...?"

"Anoki," the younger woman said. She smiled broadly, displaying a deep dimple in her right cheek. "My name is Anoki, and, um, yeah, I would love a cup of coffee."

"Nice to meet you, Anoki," she said. "My name is Bear."

"Oh, cool! Great name." Anoki nodded and walked under the shade of the tree toward the door. She peered through the pass-through and grinned. "I can see that."

Bear handed Anoki her coffee through the pass-through. "See what?" she asked.

"You're totally, like, a bear spirit," she replied. "My name is my spirit name too." She pulled a pack of American Spirits from her pocket and sat on the bench under the tree.

"What does it mean?" asked Bear.

"Well, um... my dad named me. He's part Chero-kee." Anoki pulled a long drag on her cigarette. "It's Apache for 'friend.'" She laughed. "So... I guess we'll probably be friends."

"I'd like that," Bear said and returned to the griddle. She laughed quietly. It would be just like Nonna to send someone like Anoki her way.

Chapter 8

Bear left the pink house the next morning feeling light and happy. It was a beautiful Sunday morning, and she had already been to the beach, watched the surfers, and looked for marked turtle nests. But when she pulled into the parking lot of Les Beans Café and saw Ronnie's blue BMW in the first parking space, her heart dropped. Ronnie stepped out of her car as Bear pulled in. She leaned on the hood, her arms crossed. Dressed in dark blue sweatpants and a T-shirt with her hair pulled back under a cap, she looked more like an undercover cop than a medical professional.

Ronnie launched right in without a hello. "So you think you can just walk out like that and drop all your responsibilities?"

"What are you talking about?" Bear felt a tremor begin in her throat.

"I'm talking about the house we own together." Ronnie stepped closer. "The mortgage, the bills. You think you can just walk away?" She unfolded her arms to make a sweeping motion. "Then you block my calls and don't tell me where you've moved?" She edged closer to Bear, her hands on her hips, an imposing shadow.

Bear's breath moved as unevenly as her thoughts. She was unable to form sentences, confused by Ronnie's questions. Finally, she willed herself to breathe, to focus and find words.

"What would you have done if Isabel had said yes?" she asked, surprised by the pointedness of her own question.

"I would have bought you out," Ronnie said, her eyes keen and focused. "Set it up so you could start a new life." Ronnie's face contorted when she said *start a new life.* She didn't look angry anymore. She looked sad. "I would have done it the right way," she murmured.

"The right way?" Bear repeated without thinking.

Ronnie slumped back on her car and heaved a sigh.

"People make binding agreements in good faith," she said, just above a whisper. "Especially if they claim to love each other."

"You never loved me," Bear whispered back.

Ronnie shook her head in disbelief. "Maybe the truth is you never loved *me*," she said. "You forget, Adelina, I *saw* you with Marabella, and you've never once looked at me the way you looked at her."

The memory flooded back to Bear—her birthday party at the Irish pub on 211th Street and Broadway. Ronnie had flown up and joined Bear's small group of friends. Marabella was not expected and had surprised Bear when she stopped by briefly to bring a small gift—a glass paperweight with a mother whale and her calf inside. Bear could not hide how happy she was to see Marabella, and this was not missed by anyone, though Ronnie had never said a word about it. Until now.

"Never once," she was saying, blinking back crocodile tears, "did you look at me like that, no matter how long I waited. I thought maybe when we moved to Florida things would change. I thought when I helped you open this place, things would change. But they never did, and you know it, Adelina."

"Hey, are you open?" came a voice just behind Ronnie.

Startled, Ronnie spun around and scanned Anoki from her head to her bare feet. "What do *you* want?" she spat.

"Coffee!" Anoki approached with an empty mug and a wide, dimpled grin.

"Hey, Anoki." Bear exhaled a sigh and smiled. "I'll be right there."

"You *know* her?" Ronnie asked.

"I need to get to work, Ronnie," Bear said, reaching in her pocket for the key to the café.

"Why haven't you told me where you're living?" Ronnie asked as Bear pulled the door open. "You can't just disappear, Adelina!" she shouted as Bear disappeared inside.

"So, that's your... um..." Anoki stuttered a few minutes later, as she stirred several spoonfuls of sugar into her coffee.

"Ex," answered Bear. She wondered if Anoki's sugar overload was caused by the scene she had just interrupted.

"Oh, good," Anoki said, nodding. "'Cause if that was your, like, partner, I'd be like... whoa!"

"Thanks for stepping in, Anoki."

"Aw, yeah, no problem. I was watching from the van, and it was pretty intense." She raised her brimming mug slowly to her lips and took a sip. "She called you by another name."

"Adelina." Bear nodded. "My birth name. She never called me Bear," she said. "Well, almost never."

"Yeah, I'm glad my dad named me," Anoki said, pulling out her pack of smokes and walking toward the door. "My mom wanted to name me Elizabeth." She pointed an unlit cigarette at herself. "Do I look like an Elizabeth to you?"

Bear laughed. "Not even close."

As Anoki headed back to her van, Bear stirred the onion and garlic in a large electric pan and added freshly diced tomatoes. Nonna's minestrone was the soup special today, and Bear got lost in the aroma of the kitchen, the sound of her knife chopping carrots and celery on the cutting board, the scent of the rosemary and sage as she pulled leaves from their sturdy stems. She breathed in the crisp scent of chopped parsley and slowed her breath into a patient rhythm as she plucked the tiny leaves of thyme from their thin, tender stems. Bear added each ingredient with reverence. She sprinkled the soup with salt and remembered watching Nonna do the same. *Salt is magic, Little Bear,* Nonna had said. *It heals us and protects us. Salt lives in all God's creations, in our blood and tears, our oceans. Salt is life! Without it, life has no flavor.*

The ring of Bear's cell phone pierced her reverie, and the name on the Caller ID shocked her. Beth never called. With four children, a demanding job, and a husband, phone calls from her sister were rare.

But Beth was astonishingly casual, as if in defiance of the fact that they never spoke. "Hey, Bear," she said. "How are you?"

Bear wondered how much she should tell Beth.

"Working through some challenges, but I'm OK overall."

"That's why I'm calling, actually," Beth began. "I heard you were breaking up with Ronnie, and I couldn't believe it. I had to call and find out for myself."

"Yes," Bear said firmly, "I am." She gritted her teeth and closed her eyes as if to brace herself for what was coming. Ronnie must have gotten around to her sister before she could. Just like New York, she thought, when she was talked out of walking away. But that was then.

"Bear, I don't want to sound... lecture-y... but Ronnie's, like, the best girlfriend you've ever had. Why are you doing this?"

Bear squeezed her eyes shut again. "How did you find out about this, Beth?"

Beth huffed out a breath, then confessed. "Ronnie called, and she was very, very upset. Are you having an affair or something? She thinks you may be having an affair."

"No, I am not having an affair," Bear said. "*Ronnie* has been having the affair."

"She told me she proposed to you! She gave you a ring and everything!"

"None of that was real," said Bear.

"How could that not be real?"

Bear sighed.

"OK, OK," Beth conceded. "Let's say you have some... *complaints* about your relationship. Let's say you two may have some issues to work out. Who doesn't? All I'm saying is, before you make any permanent decisions, just think about what you are walking away from. Women like Ronnie don't come around every day, Bear."

Bear sighed again. *And so it begins.* The family who hadn't accepted anyone until Ronnie showed up now wanted to weigh in because Ronnie had checked all *their* boxes. Good-looking. Professional. Wealthy. House in Boca. All the necessary credentials to counterbalance the lesbian thing. Ronnie cancelled out their embarrassment.

Months later, when Bear had experienced all of what was to come, all that would challenge her decision, challenge her new home, her safety, and the very survival of Les Beans Café, she would liken this conversation to an annoying fly in the house. The other challenges, the ones to come, were like arsonists lighting the house on fire.

"I just met Anoki," Sophie exclaimed that afternoon, all smiles at the counter. "She was helping Simon hose down the sidewalk across the street. Simon says hi, by the way."

"Hey!" Bear couldn't hide her surprise, much less how happy she was to see Sophie. "I wasn't expecting you to drop in!"

"Should I have called ahead?"

Bear laughed and shook her head.

"Well, I just came from the beach," Sophie continued. "Had to check on our babies."

"Oh?" Bear leaned toward Sophie. "I just checked on them this morning, myself." When she saw how Sophie beamed at this, she added, "How are the little darlings?"

"Napping."

Bear smiled and thought of possible responses—all of them too flirty. While her face did indeed light up in Sophie's presence and her heart did feel like an overexcited puppy, Bear knew Sophie would hardly be impressed with flirty one-liners. Flirting seemed too coarse for Sophie, like watering a beautiful flower with the hose set on full instead of a gentle mist.

"It's nice to see you," she said instead. "Would you like a breve latte?" Bear couldn't help but remember Sophie's request for a breve latte on the evening she had come out to help, and how embarrassed she had been that she did not know what a breve latte was. Sophie had graciously explained.

A flush rose in Sophie's smiling cheeks. "Thank you, but no. I'll just have some water." She placed a large, white flower on the counter.

"For you," she said. "It's a magnolia. There's a tree up the road." She leaned in close and added in a conspiratorial whisper, "I stole it."

"It's beautiful," Bear murmured, sotto voce. "I won't tell a soul." She filled a water glass and a cappuccino cup with water from the pitcher, then slid the glass to Sophie and the cup toward the magnolia flower.

"A magnolia flower is a symbol of eternal connection," Sophie was saying. "It's a favorite in wedding bouquets."

Bear paused as she placed the magnolia stem in its makeshift vase. "Are you proposing?" she asked, eyebrows raised.

"Well, I've come with a proposal, but not that kind," said Sophie, the color in her cheeks rising again. "I hope that's not too disappointing."

Bear laughed. "I'm crushed. Truly."

"I wanted to help you celebrate your new home so, my proposal—the disappointing one—is to bring over some food on your day off and help you bless your home," she said and took a sip of water. "A home isn't really a home until you've had your first guest."

"Is that a thing?"

Sophie grinned and took another sip. "No, I just made it up."

Bear laughed. "Hey, do you play piano?" she asked.

"Yes!" Sophie exclaimed, surprised. "Why?"

"I have a grand piano sitting in my living room, and I don't know how to play."

"How exciting," Sophie said. "Do you know what kind it is?"

"Not really," Bear said, trying to remember what the panel behind the keys had said. "I think it begins with a B."

"A Blüthner?"

"I guess?"

"Oh my!" said Sophie, taking her last sip of water and backing toward the door. "Well, let me know when it's good for you, and we'll bless your new home together."

Bear needed very little time to think about it.

"How's tomorrow?"

Shortly after Don Victorio's Produce market had opened on Monday morning, Bear stood in the narrow aisle by a mound of plum tomatoes and checked her list. A Spanish love song played over the speakers, and the man trimming the cabbages with a machete sang along. She had woken early this morning, smiling before she opened her eyes, and cheerily set about the usual Monday tasks of shopping, restocking, and cleaning. She paid in cash, loaded the car, and headed back to Les Beans, anxious to finish her chores, get home, and prepare for Sophie's visit.

After restocking produce, supplies, and coffee, Bear worked her way through the café, mopping the floors, scrubbing down the bathroom, replenishing the toilet paper and paper towel dispensers.

Finally, the only thing left on her list was the coffee bean order. Bear pulled out her phone and found the number for the supplier, but today Leslie in customer service sounded different than her usual cheery self.

"Your card doesn't seem to be going through, Bear," she said and offered to try it again. "Maybe it was a glitch."

The card failed a second time.

"That's really weird, Leslie," said Bear. "Let me give you the debit card then, and I'll sort that out for next time."

But the debit card didn't work either.

"That's impossible," muttered Bear.

"Does anyone else have access to your account, sweetie?"

Bear sat up and looked around the room in disbelief. She felt a rush of adrenaline to her gut and limbs. Ronnie.

"I'm sorry about this, Leslie," she said. "What are my options here?"

"We'd be happy to do a COD."

Bear hung up with a sinking feeling. If Ronnie had put a hold on their only business credit card and drained the Les Beans account, Bear would have to pay cash for everything until she could sort things out. One thing was certain: it wasn't safe to deposit another dollar in that account if Ronnie had access to it.

"I thought a picnic would be nice," Sophie said, reaching into a large, stuffed cloth bag, pulling out containers and placing them on the coffee table. She had arrived right on time and parallel-parked her old Saturn wagon on the street in front of Bear's house. She wore a white tunic with an embroidered collar that made the turquoise beads on her necklace and the red feather attached to it even more striking.

"Whoa, that's a lot of olives!" Bear enthused as she watched Sophie open an armada of deli containers. When Sophie's bag was finally empty, their coffee table picnic included a colorful and aromatic spread of black olives, kalamata olives, green olives, garlic-stuffed olives, and cheese-stuffed olives, as well as a bowl of figs, a loaf of Italian bread, dipping oil, and a bottle of chianti.

"My nonna grew a fig tree in her backyard," Bear said after biting into one of the cold, sweet fruits. "From a seed she brought from Italy."

Sophie nodded and dipped a piece of bread in the oil. "My grandfather grew chamomile." She laughed under her breath as an old memory came to her, seemingly from nowhere. "I remember visiting Grandpa and Grandma as a child, and I noticed that they took an afternoon nap together every day. If I was there when they came out of their room, I'd always pick up this scent around them that I didn't recognize." She laughed. "It wasn't until I was older that I figured it out."

"Wow," Bear laughed. "To be that in love for life..." She picked up a cheese-stuffed olive and took a little bite.

Sophie's eyes moved to the stained glass hummingbirds and for a moment seemed lost there.

"I think the deepest kind of love is when two souls find each other," she said. She became still, as if her thoughts had moved far out of reach and she waited for them to return. "They may have traveled the entire universe to find each other again. It may have taken eons." She shrugged and shook her head. "They might not even recognize each other at first, but when they do..."

"What?" Bear asked, mesmerized by her musings.

"It's a love so big, so beyond comprehension that it cracks their hearts open."

"That sounds beautiful and terrifying at the same time."

"Only because we don't know where it's going or where it came from or how it's even possible," Sophie replied. She grinned at her next thought. "Like being inside a miracle."

Bear smiled softly in return. "Have you ever felt that?"

"I thought I had," said Sophie. "Now I'm not so sure." She took a sip of her wine. "Have you?"

"I don't think so," Bear replied. "I was crazy about Marabella, but it didn't feel like that."

Sophie chuckled. "Like a heart-cracking love as deep and mysterious as the ocean?"

"Yeah," said Bear with a smile. "But I'd like to one day."

Sophie took a long sip from her glass. "Careful what you wish for, Turtle Bear."

This time Sophie's gaze held Bear in the kaleidoscopic movement of her honey brown eyes, and tilted Bear's senses as if tilting a planet on its axis to draw it closer. Later, Bear would create a fantasy of this moment in which she saw herself pushing aside the coffee table that sat between them—olives and wine flying everywhere—before lifting Sophie to her feet and kissing her deeply. In it, Sophie clung to her, swept up in her own passion, unable and unwilling to break away from their kiss.

Instead, Bear sat frozen under Sophie's gaze and pinched her thigh through her jeans until it hurt.

The sun had slipped away, and the nighttime sky appeared behind the hummingbird window. Their conversation flowed with a kind of ease that seemed to erase all sense of time. Sophie told the story of her first girlfriend and how she'd had to leave her home at seventeen. She lived in a tree for a while, she said, and showered at the beach. Bear shared a similar story. She had moved out of her home before graduating high school for the same reason. The only family member at her graduation was Nonna, who simply said, "This is how God made you, Little Bear, and so you are beautiful and perfect."

Sophie sat at the piano and ran her fingers over the keys, then the fallboard and music rack. She adjusted the piano bench and touched the pedals lightly with the toes of her sneakers.

"Tonight's concert," she began with a giggle, "is in honor of Bear's new home and new life."

Later, Bear would remember Sophie introducing Debussy's "Rêverie."

"Beautiful," Bear had whispered from the sofa where she lay. She closed her eyes and let the notes drift around her. When Sophie played another tune, ethereal and sad, Bear asked, "Who is this?"

"Me," said Sophie. "It's an improvisation."

Bear wanted to ask Sophie if she felt as sad as the music she played, but sleep pulled her away into a dream and the music drifted into echoes.

Bear did not see, as Sophie did, a shadow cross the window below the hummingbirds. She did not hear the music stop nor hear Sophie move to the front door and step out into the night to breathe the air, searching for the scent of the intruder. She did not hear the soft clatter of dishes in the kitchen or feel the blanket when Sophie covered her, and Bear did not feel the kiss on her forehead when Sophie departed.

Les Beans was packed for a Tuesday evening, and Bear was relieved. She needed every dollar of tonight's revenue for the coffee order arriving to-morrow.

Linda and Micki had arrived early and offered to help with drink orders if Bear found herself in the weeds.

"I cannot believe," Micki had gushed, "that Deb-bie the Dominatrix is coming to Les Beans tonight!"

Bear almost couldn't believe it either. According to Micki, Debbie was wildly popular at the girl bars in Fort Lauderdale. When Debbie had called to in-quire about hosting a bingo night at Les Beans Café, Bear explained that Les Beans did not serve alco-hol, so she would not be able to pay her.

"Listen, precious," Debbie had replied, "I charge five dollars a card and put out a tip jar. The rest is all you. I'll promote whatever you're serving, and if

I don't see drinks in front of them, I'll put 'em on the rack. Besides," she added, more seriously, "I'm looking forward to a sober crowd."

Now the room erupted into whoops and shouts as Debbie mounted the stage. "Hellooooo, Lez Beeeeeeeaaaans!" she shouted into the microphone. Debbie wore a patent-leather bustier over knee-high black boots and a black cat-eye mask. She held a cat-o'-nine tales in her right hand. "Thanks for coming out tonight for Bingo Night with Debbie the Dominatrix. Y'all look beautiful!"

The crowd cheered, and she grinned knowingly into the spotlight.

"That's right, soak it up. Once the game begins, I'm going to be a total bitch to you. But I heard some of you like that. OK, so the prizes tonight are gift certificates to one of my favorite pleasure stores. I want to see drinks and food on your tables too. We gotta support this place."

The event ended promptly at ten o'clock, and most of Debbie's fans filed out. A few stayed behind to mingle, and one fan, a young woman with long, wild, dark hair, wearing an *Edward Scissorhands* T-shirt, hovered close to Debbie onstage. It looked like she was untying Debbie's bustier. Debbie didn't seem to mind.

"Who is that?" asked Bear, pointing with her chin toward the stage as Micki approached the counter.

"That's Toni," said Micki. "She follows Debbie all over South Florida. Shows up at all her events." Linda and Bear laughed and watched Toni straddle Debbie on a chair and pantomime to Björk's "Big Time Sensuality."

"The aftershow!" Linda laughed.

"Is she...?" Bear stared at Toni, who now gyrated over Debbie.

"Doing a lap dance?" Linda finished Bear's question. "Yes, indeedy!"

"Should I stop her?" Bear asked.

Micki laughed. "Debbie's the one with the whip, Bear."

"Well," Bear sighed, "this is a first for Les Beans." Her attention shifted to Linda and Micki, who were leaning into each other, Linda's hand placed tenderly on Micki's back. "You two are really cute together, by the way," she said.

Micki turned and leaned over the counter toward Bear. "Wouldn't we make cute babies?" she asked. Bear glanced at Linda, who tilted her head out of view and grimaced.

"Adorable," Bear chimed in, tickled by Linda's squirming.

Debbie gathered her materials and approached the counter. "I had a lovely time, ladies," she said with a toothy smile. "Let me know when you'd like to do this again, Bear."

"Thank you, Debbie," Bear said and extended her hand. "It was a great night for the café too. I'd love to have you back." Bear knew before counting the drawer that she would have plenty for the coffee delivery in the morning. With more nights like this, she could expand her lunch menu, too.

"We're off, too," Linda said, taking Micki by the hand. "You good, Bear?"

"Yeah," she said. "I'll be out of here in a few." She stood in the kitchen and counted out the drawer, putting aside the cash she needed for the coffee delivery, then counting the surplus. Nearly one hundred dollars. Plenty to buy the spices and other ingredients needed for next week's soup specials. A wave of excitement washed over her. She was one step closer to her vision...

"Hey!" A voice pierced the silence of the kitchen. Toni, the would-be lap dancer, had stuck her head through the pass-through. "Do you know this woman out here in the van?"

Bear laughed out loud. Toni looked a bit silly with her head poked awkwardly through the pass-through, like an exuberant watchdog.

"That's Anoki," she said. "She's a friend."

Toni gave a nod and grinned. "Cool!"

Bear sat at the stoplight and turned to watch the waxing moon rise over the ocean. She thought of the beautiful piano notes that had lulled her to sleep the night before, the sight of Sophie dipping her bread in olive oil and her gravitational gaze. She let her mind wander to her fantasy of the coffee table being flipped and to that imagined kiss.

The ring of Bear's phone pierced her daydream and made her heart jump. As she reoriented herself in her surroundings, she wondered who would be calling her this late.

Sophie's voice was tender, and it felt as though Bear's thoughts had summoned her. "I'm just checking on you," she intimated. Bear's cheeks flushed when she imagined Sophie peeking into her daydream.

"Where are you?" Sophie asked.

"I'm on my way home," said Bear. "That's very sweet of you to ask." She turned down Lakeside.

"I wanted to make sure you got home safely," Sophie said.

"Are you worried about me?" Bear asked, knowing her question was more subtly flirtatious than serious. For once she didn't care, emboldened as she was by her own daydream.

Sophie did not answer.

"Where are you now?" she asked again.

"Just pulling into my driveway," Bear said as she turned off the engine.

"Good," said Sophie. "Then you are home safe."

Bear sat still, listening. Sophie sounded more like a lover than a friend tonight, and Bear wanted to keep her on the phone.

"I appreciate your concern, Soph—wait..."

Bear's voice broke off as two shadowy figures emerged from behind the garage and moved swiftly toward her car, one approaching her window, the other moving to the passenger side. Dazed, she followed the man, now at her window, whose face was covered in a bandana, who pointed a gun at her head. His left hand pounded on her window.

"Open the door!" he shouted.

"Is this a joke?" Bear asked in disbelief.

Thud! Thud! Thud! The sound from the passenger-side window reverberated through the car.

The man at the passenger window held his pointed gun with both hands, his eyebrows turned inward over his own bandana-covered face.

"Open the door," the first gunman ordered a second time. Bear cracked opened her door, and the gunman pulled the handle, swinging it wide.

"Give me your bag," he growled.

Bear handed him the backpack, her mind, still in shock, moving in slow motion.

"Give me your phone," he ordered, and Bear realized she had never hung up. The man reached in and took the phone from her hand. In a flash, both men disappeared into the darkness. An engine started on the next street, and a car screeched off at great speed.

The thought came to her slowly. *They were waiting for me.*

Bear stumbled out of the car and doubled over on the lawn. Shock and terror traveled together in an expanding ball, up through her lungs and throat as if she had just woken from a nightmare to discover it was real, every bit of it. The men waiting behind the garage. The guns. The masks. As surreal and dreamlike as it felt, it was all real, and she couldn't even call for help. Her sobs sounded foreign to her in the darkness. She staggered to the nearest house and rang the bell. No one answered.

Patricia Lucia

She ran to another and another until finally a young couple opened their door and stood wide-eyed in the doorway.

"Please, help me," she sobbed.

Chapter 9

Bear did not know that, in the moments she stood frozen on the front lawn of her new home, Sophie stood in her own bedroom five miles north, her phone in hand, having heard the terrible thud on Bear's car window and the gunman's pointed order. She did not know that Sophie's fears had unfolded before her, in the guise of an audio recording of a crime she could not stop, and that Sophie had listened until the phone went dead in the gunman's hands. Bear did not know that even as the police arrived and cordoned off the block, even as the detective listened to Bear's stuttered description and made careful notes, that it was Sophie who had made that first call to the police and that by the time Bear had gotten to a neighbor's phone, the police were already on their way. So was Sophie.

Bear stood on the front steps with an officer who had introduced himself as Detective Hurley.

He had just completed his report and was assuring Bear one of his colleagues would be posted out front for the night.

"Just one last question," the detective said. "Do you know anyone who might want to do you harm?"

Bear had sensed this question coming during their interview. The two assailants appeared to be gang members but did not exhibit gang-like behavior during the robbery, the detective had noted. They had been waiting for her—a planned attack—but they did not take her car. They did not drag her into the house and assault her—or worse. They didn't hit her or even call her names. And while this was all extremely fortunate for Bear, it didn't add up.

"Why don't you give it some thought and call me if you think of anything," he said and handed Bear his card.

Hurley was in the middle of making suggestions about ways to stay safe as a business owner coming home late at night when Sophie's car pulled up. Sophie burst out and strode across the lawn, cutting between the detective and Bear and interrupting his instructions in mid-sentence. Bear welcomed Sophie's fierce embrace and, despite her best efforts not to, collapsed onto Sophie's shoulder and sobbed.

"They said I couldn't cross the barrier," Sophie breathed, "but I told them I was the one who called, and I needed—" Her voice broke off. "I needed to see you. I needed to see you with my own eyes."

The first light of morning streamed through the east-facing window of Bear's bedroom as she emerged from a long dream and became conscious of the fact that she lay fully clothed and curled like a child on top of her covers. She listened to her breath. Her hand was still curled under her chin, and the fine hairs along her forearm registered the faint movement of a breath that was not hers.

Bear opened her eyes. Sophie lay on her side, her face close to Bear's, as if she had fallen asleep while speaking. She may have. The last thing Bear remembered was Sophie's assurance that she could close her eyes and sleep.

The sunlight pooled on Sophie's cheek and along her brow and eyelashes. She still wore her jeans and the T-shirt Bear had sobbed into and those yellow socks with tuxedo cats leaping across the toes, the one thing that had made Bear smile last night.

A thought came to Bear and brought with it a prickly shadow of fear. What if Sophie had not come? What if there was no Sophie at all? Who would she have called? Where could she have gone? Bear's breath quickened, and Sophie opened her eyes.

"Are you OK?" she whispered.

Bear felt tears behind her eyes. "Thank you for being here," she murmured.

Sophie smiled and pulled Bear's hand from under her chin and held it. "You're welcome, but you didn't answer my question."

"I was thinking—" Bear's voice caught in her throat, and her eyes became blurry. "I was thinking about being alone in the world."

Sophie nodded. "We're never really alone in the world, Bear, even when we think we are."

Bear let her tears slide onto the pillow.

"Like my nonna," she whispered.

Sophie smiled. "Yes," she whispered. "Like Nonna." Bear felt Sophie's fingers on her wet cheek, then her hand on her shoulder. She let herself curl up in Sophie's arms.

"Have I told you about how I learned to swim?" Sophie asked.

Bear lay with her head buried under Sophie's chin, breathing in her scent and listening to the soft thump of her heart.

"No," she murmured.

"Well," Sophie began, "I remember it had been quite stormy and the waves were large and ominous. My father took me out on the rocks of the jetty to watch the water crashing and churning like a washing machine. Or so he said. The next thing I knew, my father had thrown me into the wild waters below us."

Bear frowned. "Why?"

Sophie laughed. "Later, after I had made it to shore and stopped crying, he told me he was teaching me how to swim and how to live."

Hours later, Bear sat in the café's kitchen, staring at the phone and rehearsing how she was going to tell Ronnie about the robbery. She had not wanted to tell her at all but felt Nonna's nudge that it would be the right thing to do. Finally, she picked up the phone and heard herself say the words that still felt unreal.

"I was robbed at gunpoint last night, Ronnie," she said and braced herself for Ronnie's reaction. She waited several moments in silence.

"That's why I would never live in that neighborhood," Ronnie finally said, her voice distant, matter-of-fact.

"That's it?" Bear couldn't help demanding.

"What?" Ronnie asked.

147

"I was robbed at gunpoint last night, and all you have to say is you're glad you don't live in my neighborhood?!"

"This is what you wanted, Adelina," she said. "Did you call the police?"

"Of course I did," said Bear. "And filed a report with a detective."

"What did the detective say about it?"

"He thinks someone may have wanted to harm me or scare me," Bear said.

Ronnie was silent for a few moments. "Huh."

Bear sat still and silent for a long time after the call, her mind moving back and forth between thoughts, unable to touch any deeper than the surface of what they presented. If she allowed her thoughts to linger long enough on the unthinkable, she could neither escape nor deny the shadowy reality that she had chosen, years ago when she believed she was stepping into a safer existence: a more secure and stable life with Ronnie. She had known Ronnie was controlling, and Ronnie could be cruel. But would she orchestrate such pointed malevolence? Intend such terror? To entertain this possibility was to accept her own hand in it. After all, she had bound herself to Ronnie. Moved away from all that was familiar for a life with her. Made promises and commitments.

So Bear pushed aside any thought that Ronnie had had a hand in the robbery, not because she wished to protect Ronnie from such unforgivable choices, but because she could not yet Bear the weight of her own.

The café door swung open under the clanging bell as Linda and Micki stomped in.

"What the hell, Bear Bear!" Linda's voice rang out. "Are you all right? I heard what happened."

Micki trailed behind her with wide eyes. "Yeah!" she echoed. "What the hell!"

Bear assured them she had not been harmed and that Sophie had made sure she had gotten rest.

"Sophie said she saw someone creeping your yard around the night before," said Linda.

"Yeah," said Bear. "I was asleep when that happened."

Linda and Micki exchanged glances, and Linda leaned on the counter to rest her chin on her palm.

"Mm," she murmured. "She said you two had a *picnic?*"

Bear grinned. "It was a house blessing." She felt a flush rising in her cheeks.

"Come to think of it, baby," Micki said, turning to Linda, "we've been blessing the shit out of my house this week."

149

"So are you OK, Bear Bear?" Linda asked, ignoring Micki.

"I guess so," Bear said. "The detective suspects it wasn't what it looked like."

"What do you mean?"

"Well, it looked like gang members were robbing me," Bear began, "but he said their behavior didn't add up. He suspects that someone wanted to scare the shit out of me."

"That's some fucked-up shit right there," Linda said, slapping her hand on the counter.

"Yeah," Micki echoed. "That's fucked-up."

"Well, it worked." Bear nodded. "I was terrified." Then she remembered how she had gotten through the night. "I don't know what I would have done if Sophie hadn't shown up."

"Ouch!" exclaimed Linda. "Good friend standing right here. Don't ever hesitate to call me, Bear Bear."

"That's right!" echoed Micki. "Don't hesitate!"

"I'm glad Sophie was there, though," said Linda, after cutting Micki a *Would you cut it out already?* stare. "And I can see it with you two. You're both kinda weird in the same way."

Bear laughed. It was true. But Sophie was special in ways Bear could not begin to explain. She felt more like a dream than a person sometimes. Bear couldn't imagine someone like Sophie falling for someone like her.

"Hey, Bear," Micki cut into her thoughts, "I have a question for you, 'cause this one"—she nodded toward Linda—"won't answer me."

"Oh, boy," Linda muttered under her breath.

"So we were talking about how cute our baby would look," Micki began. Linda put her head down on the counter. "And *she* said if I had her baby it would look like a cornbread baby."

Linda snort-laughed into the counter.

"Do you know what that means?" Micki asked. "She won't tell me."

Micki's own brand of weirdness tickled Bear, and she laughed despite the earnest look on Micki's face.

"I have no idea, Micki," she said.

"Did you know," Linda asked, changing the subject, "that Micki is adopted?"

Bear looked at Micki, who nodded enthusiastically

"Linda said I should do one of those DNA tests," she said, "so I can find my biological family. She's going to do it with me."

"That sounds exciting," said Bear. "And romantic."

"Yeah, well," said Linda, with a raised brow. "This all goes south if we find out that she has alien DNA." She turned to Micki. "You can't have my cornbread kid if you're an alien, babe."

In the kitchen the next morning, Bear opened a fresh container of berbere spice and breathed it in, the notes of chili pepper tickling her nose. Berbere—a rich, orange-red collection of roasted paprika, fenugreek, coriander, cumin, and cardamom—was the centerpiece of Ethiopian red lentil stew, the day's soup special. Bear chopped the onion and garlic and diced the potatoes. In a separate bowl she had collected the ingredients for a batch of naan. The Ethiopian red lentil stew always sold out, especially when it was served with warm bread.

Surprised by a knock on the kitchen door, Bear absently thought it might be Anoki, parked again under the mango tree, but when she opened the door, a middle-aged man in a white-collared, city-issued shirt stood on the other side of the screen with a clipboard.

"Good morning," he said. "Are you the owner of this establishment?"

"Yes," Bear replied, eying the clipboard.

"My name is Jeff O'Connor," he said and smiled pleasantly. "I'm an inspector with the City of Lake Worth. I'm just following up on a few complaints we have received about your business."

"Complaints?" Bear asked. She couldn't imagine what violations Les Beans could have made.

"May I step in?"

"Of course," said Bear, opening the screen door. "Can I get you a cup of coffee?"

O'Connor paused and pressed his lips together. "You know what, I'd love a cup," he said. "And whatever you're making in here smells delicious. I could smell it in the parking lot."

A few moments later, Bear and O'Connor sat at a table for their discussion.

"So whenever someone makes a complaint," O'Connor began, "we are obligated to follow up."

"I understand," said Bear. She was watching his face and saw an ordinary, kindhearted man. As nerve-racking as this felt, Bear saw no malice or ill intention in him. She suspected it came from another source.

"So the complaints are," O'Connor was saying as he flipped through his papers, "serving alcohol on the premises."

Bear's eyes widened.

"Allowing individuals to live in this establishment," he continued.

"What?" she whispered.

O'Connor looked up briefly and read on. "Cutting hair on the premises."

Bear tilted her head and frowned.

"And allowing patrons to enter a food establishment with bare feet." O'Connor chuckled at the last complaint. "We do live in a beach town, after all."

"Mr. O'Connor—"

"Call me Jeff."

"Jeff, these complaints are fabrications," Bear said. "But how am I supposed to prove that?"

"So none of this has happened here?"

Bear took a breath and sighed. "One night after closing, I shared a bottle of wine with two friends."

"If no money was exchanged, that's perfectly OK," said Jeff.

"It wasn't. And I have a customer who is a traveler," continued Bear. "She's parked her van outside overnight a couple of times."

"Does she live in her van?" Jeff asked.

"Yes."

"That's also perfectly OK."

"And I have no idea about the haircutting." Bear shook her head. "Maybe Anoki—the girl who lives in her van—maybe she trimmed her hair in the parking lot or something. I just don't know."

Jeff laughed. "That sounds about right," he said.

"You can't tell me who made the complaints?"

"No," he said. "Do you think someone would want to hurt your business?"

"Yes," she said.

Jeff checked his papers and looked up. "Does this person live in Boca? This looks like a Boca number."

Bear's eyes widened. "Yes."

"Who lives in Boca?"

Bear swallowed. Saying it out loud made it too real.

"My ex."

Days later, Bear found herself running full tilt in the rain down the alley from Les Beans to the utilities building two blocks over on Main Street, the electric bill in her left pocket and the exact amount of cash tucked in her right pocket. If the past due amount wasn't paid today, the customer service person had said, the electricity would be turned off tomorrow. Most of the surrounding towns had gone digital for utilities payments, but Lake Worth still

155

held to three forms of payment: mail, drive-through, and in-person.

Bear jumped puddles along the two blocks between the café and the utilities building, skipped up the steps to the glass door, and exhaled she was once inside, rain dripping off her poncho onto the long, black doormat. The electric bill had nearly doubled in the hot summer months while the café, like most businesses in town, had gotten slower. Bear had been forced to dip into her tip money to cover this bill.

"Guess I don't need to ask if it's raining outside," said the clerk behind the plexiglass. She smiled, showing a gap between her front teeth. The woman seemed ageless, with smooth, dark skin and locs that grew to her shoulders, lightly brushed with gray and scattered with cowry shells.

Bear laughed. "If I had waited for the sun to come out, my electricity would have been cut off."

"I hear you," the clerk replied, her voice deep and rich. "That café on the corner yours?"

"Yes," Bear said.

"Cute place," she said, counting out the bills Bear had slid under the plexiglass. "Gone by a couple of times."

"Thank you."

The woman looked familiar, but Bear could not place her face. Then she remembered the people she had seen fishing under the bridge. "I think I've seen you fishing at the bridge."

The clerk looked up and grinned. "That's right!" she said. "I try to get out as much as I can and fish the incoming tide."

"Ah," said Bear. "You are a dedicated fisher-woman."

The clerk laughed. "There's a reason," she said, sliding Bear's receipt under the plexiglass, "that Jesus hung out with fishermen."

"Why is that?" Bear smiled. She felt like she could listen to this woman all day.

"The ocean holds all the answers, baby," the clerk said with that same wide grin. "Every time I eat a fish that's been swimming around in it, I feel like I've solved another mystery."

Lunches at Les Beans Café grew brisker at summer's end, as word got out about the homemade soups and herbed naan bread Bear made fresh every day. She developed a daily routine, rising early and arriving hours before opening. She prepared the lunch special, stacked cups, cleaned the espresso machine, checked her milk supply, cleaned the bathroom, and labeled and restocked the coffee. And every morning between eight thirty and nine, the little flip phone she had purchased after the robbery chimed with a message from Sophie.

How is your heart today, Bear?

Good morning! You will be happy to know that more of our babies have flown the nest (with their little flippers) and are now flying the oceans.

This rain! Are you puddle-jumping today? (I hope so. They say it's good for the heart.)

What magic are you stirring up in your kitchen today?

Bear's favorite messages were those that promised a visit.

I've made corn chowder and would love to bring you a cup. (To get your professional opinion, of course.)

But Bear would remember most fondly the message she received on a Wednesday morning in October. This particular message presented an invitation of which she thought herself unworthy, and yet for which she had secretly yearned.

I would like to invite you to dinner at my home this weekend, Sophie had texted. *Would you like that?*

The invitation would set in motion a course for Bear's heart from which there was no return, and while Bear had no way of knowing any of this at the time, she *felt* it. She felt it in the sudden rushes of joy that moved through her body and made her giddy, the tug at her heart that felt vaguely like a muscle being stretched, and the feeling that all her senses had tilted on their axis into the gravitational pull of Sophie's beautiful planet.

Bear pulled up in front of the address Sophie had given her, a two-story cottage behind a larger house. She checked her reflection in the rearview mirror and took a breath. She wore her best faded jeans, her favorite tunic top, and sandals. She had practically scrubbed herself raw in the shower, spending extra time on her nails, which were always dirty with whatever Bear had gotten her hands into on any given day. She grabbed the bottle of cabernet she had bought at Publix and walked as casually as she could to Sophie's front door, where Sophie stood, smiling.

After welcoming Bear inside, Sophie poured a generous amount of cabernet into Bear's glass and half that amount into her own.

"I've already had some," Sophie was saying, a flush rising in her cheeks. "I think I was a little nervous."

"Me too," said Bear and smiled at the apron Sophie wore. It was a patchwork of different fabrics and colors—denim, corduroy, cotton and silk, some with swirls and flowers, paisley and stripes; some in earth tones and some with splashes of vibrant color. She followed the slow, circular motion of Sophie's hand as she stirred the contents of a small pot over a low flame.

"You never asked me about my name," Bear said as Sophie lifted the wooden spoon and blew on a red dollop of sauce.

"I would have," Sophie said, "if I had a question." She smiled and raised the spoon toward Bear's lips.

Bear let the sauce sit on her tongue and closed her eyes. She tasted the warm earthiness of the onion and garlic, the fresh tomato and red wine. The sauce had simmered for more than a day, she could tell; it was deep, rich, the ingredients fully married. But the rosemary! How it danced on her palate and lingered there, even as she spoke.

"Rosemary," she said. "My favorite."

"Mine too," Sophie said, then, after a moment, asked, "Have you read *Hamlet*?"

"Of course," Bear said, surprised.

"Ophelia." Sophie nodded.

"Only my favorite character of all time." Bear chuckled grimly. "Well, her and poor Desdemona."

"Both so courageous and tragic," Sophie said. "Do you remember what Ophelia said about rose-mary?"

"Rosemary for remembrance," Bear answered.

Sophie placed the spoon carefully on a small plate and turned the burner off. "Would you like a tour?" she asked.

"Isn't that what the complimentary wine is for?" Bear quipped, pleased to see Sophie laugh and the blush deepen in her cheeks.

The main entrance to Sophie's small cottage was through her kitchen, the heart of her home, where oregano, rosemary, and sage grew in tiny clay pots on the windowsill and baskets hung, full of onions, squash, and bananas. A complex blend of aromas hung in the air. Bear recognized the scent of cinnamon and cardamom, coffee, freshly chopped green vegetables, spiced orange, and somewhere, faintly, nag champa incense.

A wooden staircase rose steeply on the far wall of the kitchen and curved into the loft above. An arched doorway with three steps down led to a small, sunken living room lined with crowded book-shelves, a hanging guitar and mandolin on one side of a picture window and two framed albums, *Tea for the Tillerman* and *Joan Armatrading* on the other. A small piano sat in a corner with sheet music open on the rack.

"Great albums," Bear said. "Classics!"

"Timeless!" Sophie paused at the base of the stairs to the loft. She glanced up toward the darkened room and hesitated, then turned to Bear.

"Are you hungry?" she asked finally.

Sophie had baked spaghetti squash with the rich tomato sauce Bear had tasted, then topped it with melted feta cheese, a perfect complement for the strong presence of rosemary. She placed half a squash on each plate and poured more wine in their glasses.

"It's a simple meal," she said, almost shyly.

"It's perfect," said Bear.

They ate from the squash, dipping their forks and twirling the spaghetti-like strands in the chunky, dark sauce. Sophie had put an album on, with music so unusual it made Bear giggle.

"Who is this?" she asked. "I adore it."

Sophie laughed. "I thought you might," she said. "It's Joanna Newsom."

They spoke in murmurs and slurped their spaghetti squash as Joanna Newsom sang "Bridges and Balloons" in an untamed, reckless, childlike voice.

Bear wouldn't remember much of their conversation later, though she had hung on every word and had not looked away from the honey-golden kaleidoscopes of Sophie's eyes. She would remember Sophie's breathy voice in bits and pieces. Favorite recipes. Ghost stories and spirit animals. Moths and dragons. Atlantis and Machu Picchu. Giants and faeries.

"Sometimes," said Sophie, putting her empty glass down and sitting back in her chair. "Sometimes when I look at you..." Her expression changed, and her eyes grew more intent, full of moving thoughts. Bear sat still, wishing she could hear them. "Sometimes you look like you," Sophie concluded, "and sometimes you look... ancient."

"Ancient," Bear repeated.

"From another time." Sophie leaned closer. "But you always look familiar."

They sat in silence for several moments. Sophie's gaze was still crowded with thoughts, a monologue that Bear was sure she could not comprehend even if Sophie had said it out loud. She shifted in her seat and cleared her throat. She had her own swirling thoughts, thoughts that she could not hide so well behind her eyes—thoughts that would not stay silent either.

"Sometimes," Bear said, forming the words as she said them, or perhaps gathering the courage to say the words as they left the safety of her mouth. "When I look at you..." Sophie smiled at this, and Bear pressed her moist palms against her thighs. "You look... beautiful."

There. Bear had said it. She felt the heat of her words in her face. Sophie lowered her gaze. Her lashes flickered.

"And sometimes," Bear continued, surprising herself. She grinned when Sophie's gaze lifted in anticipation. "You look... like a dream."

Sophie sat frozen, eyes averted, her smile replaced with an expression Bear did not recognize. When she stood and moved toward the living room, Bear's thoughts raced to form an apology. *I'm sorry. That was forward of me.* She rubbed her palms and grimaced at her overstep.

A moment later, the record player clicked softly, and the first chords of a familiar Armatrading song filled the room. "'Love and Affection,'" Bear mused as Sophie reappeared under the arched doorway. Bear felt relieved when Sophie smiled. Perhaps she had not overstepped. But when Sophie held out her hand to dance, Bear's heart skipped a beat.

Sophie must have seen it on her face because she said, "It takes courage to dance in doorways, Bear."

Bear rubbed her palms on her jeans, rose unsteadily from her chair, and joined Sophie under the arch. Sophie's hand felt soft and warm in Bear's, and the curves of their bodies fit comfortably, breasts greeting breasts, blushed cheek touching blushed cheek. They swayed and turned easily, with the kind of familiarity of those who have danced often together. As nervous as Bear had been to be this close to Sophie, it was the touch of Sophie's body that eased her. The rise and fall of her breath became the rise and fall of Sophie's; the sway of her hips, the sway of Sophie's. They moved in a dance within a dance: the outer one to the music rising from the record player; the inner one to another rhythm, ancient and familiar, they both felt but did not yet understand.

Bear could not feel where her body ended and Sophie's began or which racing thoughts were hers and which were Sophie's. She did not know whose heart trembled or whose breath quivered. She had closed her eyes to everything but Sophie, taking her into all her senses.

The floor melted away. She could not hear the creaks of the wooden boards beneath their feet, but she felt the cool wall at her back when Sophie's body pressed against hers and when Sophie's fingers moved across her face and through her hair. Bear's eyes were still closed when Sophie kissed her lightly at first, then again when Sophie's lips trembled across the contour of her mouth, tracing it, as if to breathe Bear in before giving herself fully to a kiss that would begin a more intimate dance still. Bear knew this. Even in her own chaotic thoughts, she knew Sophie had not danced like this since she had danced with her wife, had not kissed or put her hands in another woman's hair like this.

Bear opened her eyes. Sophie's face, her kaleidoscope eyes, her mouth and brow drew bolder lines than the expression Bear had seen when she had called her beautiful. Desire itself had awakened, fresh in its flushed beauty and terrified by its own unstoppable nature. All of this lay bare in Sophie's face and, in the moments that followed, would be mirrored in her own.

Here, in the doorway, Bear's mouth and hands searched with growing urgency, as if under a vast, churning ocean, tossed and pulled in an undertow, gasping for air, grasping warm flesh, until Sophie's hand pulled her upward and higher still, toward the waves and soft linens in the room above.

Chapter 10

The smell of fresh coffee drifted up the stairs and over to the bed, where Bear lay, lingering at the edges of a dream, holding on to its fading colors and sweet faces as she departed. Returning to the cool, soft sheets of Sophie's bed, she heard the creaking of the kitchen floor below, the clink of a spoon on a saucer, and the soft pat of bare feet on the stairs. Bear's thoughts wandered back to the hours before sleep and dreams had claimed her; to the color and scent of Sophie's face, her back and slender neck, the softness of her breasts and belly, her taste and the way she moved, inviting Bear to drink from her river.

The bed moved, and Sophie leaned on the pillow next to her. Soft fingers brushed her brow and cheek. Still, Bear closed her eyes to the morning, lingering in the darkness behind her lids and the images that moved there.

"Good morning," Sophie whispered, with a smile behind her words.

"Yes," Bear replied, her eyes closed and face tilted toward Sophie.

Sophie lifted the sheet. "I think I made quite a mess last night," she said with a giggle.

"Nope," said Bear. "Didn't happen."

"No?"

Sophie's cheek felt warm on Bear's face, and she could almost taste the fresh coffee on her lips.

"Not a drop made it to the sheets," Bear insisted. Sophie flushed and giggled, then slid under the sheets again. "Can I tell you about this dream I had last night?" Bear asked as Sophie pressed her face into the crook of her neck.

"Of course," she said. "I love a good dream."

"In the dream I'm traveling," Bear began, "in an unfamiliar place. I see a path and I'm following it. I think I'm trying to get home. And I come to this large stairway that leads to a huge, fancy house. Maybe a palace. I walk up these white marble stairs into a palatial mansion, and there is a party going on. I feel out of place, but no one says anything. Everything is silver, white, and cobalt blue. The dresses women are wearing, even the chalices people are drinking from."

168

"Fancy!" whispered Sophie.

"I'm offered a drink, but I don't take it. I feel like I'm in the wrong place, so I leave and go down the marble stairs to the street again, which is kind of a dirt road. And I go a little farther down, and there is this little house, almost like a hut, really, and there are people there. The people are very humble-looking, and the men all are in their shirtsleeves, though some are wearing ties. And some of the women have babies in their arms. These people are not tall like the others, but shorter with dark, curly hair. I feel comfortable here and want to stay. The next thing I know, I'm sitting at a table across from this woman."

"Now it gets juicy," Sophie said.

"She is talking to me, and it feels very tender, loving. She is a small woman with a round face and green eyes."

"Like you," Sophie inserted. Bear smiled.

"She feels like such a gentle soul, and I know that I love her. Then it's time to go, but I don't really want to. I walk out onto the little stone path that leads to the road, and just before I get to the road, I hear applause behind me. The people in the hut are applauding me, and I think, 'How strange, to applaud someone for having come.' I turn around and see her on the stone path behind me, and I go back to her to say goodbye, and I'm feeling even more love for her than before. I lean over to kiss her because it feels right, but she holds her hand up as if to say, 'No, we're not going to kiss,' so I embrace her instead. Then I woke up."

"Do you remember anything she said?"

"No, but it felt important. Like stuff I needed to know. Bits of wisdom, maybe."

"It's a fascinating dream." Sophie nodded. "There are the two distinct places in the dream. Your choice to be in the humbler place makes sense for your life now and the choices you are making."

"What about the woman?" Bear asked. "Why wouldn't she kiss me?"

"Maybe," said Sophie, biting Bear's ear gently, "she knew I was in the next room."

Bear listened to the shower run until she heard the squeak of the faucet. She watched parts of Sophie move past the crack in the bathroom door as she sipped the last of her coffee. A rattling hum erupted on the nightstand, and Sophie's phone lit up.

"You've got a call, Sophie," Bear called across the room.

Sophie groaned. "It's probably work," she called back. "Could you see who it is?"

Bear stretched toward the nightstand and re-trieved the phone.

"Catherine," she said.

"Who?" Sophie peeked from the bathroom, scowling.

"Catherine," Bear repeated. She watched So-phie's face change and wondered why she looked frightened. "Do you want to answer it?" she asked, holding the phone toward Sophie, who stood frozen like a pillar of salt in the bathroom doorway. Bear held the phone out until it stopped ringing. Sophie exhaled.

"What's wrong?" Bear asked. "You look like you've seen a ghost."

Sophie sat on the edge of the bed. Her eyes shifted from left to right as if chasing a thought or running from one. "That was Catherine," she said, quietly.

"Yes?"

"*My* Catherine."

Sophie's words settled on Bear like volcanic ash. *Catherine*. Catherine the unforgiven. Catherine...

"Your..." Bear began but could not say it.

"Wife."

They sat in silence for several moments. A sickening dread curdled in Bear's stomach, and she was sure it would get worse if she uttered a single word.

"After all these months," Sophie was saying. She shook her head in disbelief. "All this time and she calls now."

"Are you going to call her back?" Bear asked and wondered if her voice gave away the fear tightening its grip around her throat.

Sophie buttoned her jeans and pulled on a T-shirt, then disappeared into the bathroom again. Bear listened to the buzz of Sophie's electric toothbrush, the squeak of the sink faucet and the running water, and finally, when the water had been turned off, a loud sigh that echoed off the mirror over the sink.

Sophie returned, sat down next to Bear, and leaned her head close to hers.

"You know the answer to that question, Bear," she said. When Bear lowered her eyes and nodded, Sophie cupped her cheek in her palm. "This is scary for both of us, but I need to."

Sophie disappeared down the stairs and into the kitchen, the creak of floorboards shadowing her, then the soft clink of dishes. Sophie moved to the living room and after a moment, "Wild World" played softly enough for Bear to hear Sophie's voice, low and unfamiliar, over the melancholic notes. She tried to make out Sophie's words but could only follow the timber of her voice and the way it lilted upward at the ends of her sentences, as if she was happy to hear Catherine's voice.

Bear found herself rushing to the bathroom to run the water in the sink. She needed to drown out Sophie's voice and wash her from her face and hands. It was best to pretend that this had never happened. That she had never told Sophie she was beautiful or danced in her doorway. That she had never breathed her in. That they had never kissed or made love, and most of all, that she was not already falling in love.

Hours later, after Bear had quietly slipped out of Sophie's house, after she had prepared the creamy watercress soup and naan for the day's lunch special and kept her mind and body busy through the lunchtime rush, she stood in a quiet kitchen with her hands in warm, soapy water, battling her own thoughts. She had resisted the images and sounds of her and Sophie's lovemaking only to surrender fully to them, closing her eyes and opening her senses again to the color in Sophie's cheeks, the sounds of her startled pleasure, the scent of sandalwood on her skin and the way her hand rested on Bear's face as she slept.

Earlier, while preparing the soup, Bear had felt that Nonna was close and had implored her to give some kind of assurance that she had not opened her heart only to have it wounded again. Nonna's answer had been tender, brief, and so disappointing Bear resolved not to speak of Sophie with Nonna again.

Bear had returned to the more pleasant images of the night before when her daydream was interrupted by the ringing of the bell over the front door.

Linda clunked down a brown paper bag with what looked like a pint of liquor in it and stood at the counter, hands in her pockets, staring at the package. Bear emerged from the kitchen and raised her brows.

"Hey, Linda," she greeted her, and when Linda did not look up from the paper bag, she asked, "What's going on?"

Linda sighed loudly. "I'm going to need a single-shot latte, Bear Bear. And just fill the cup halfway."

Bear prepared her drink and watched from the corner of her eye as Linda unscrewed a pint of Captain Morgan and tapped the counter nervously with the cap. She poured the rum into the mug Bear had slid toward her, took a long sip, and poured more.

"Bear Bear," she said, finally looking up, "I'd ask you which news you want to hear first, the good news or the bad news, but not today." She stopped to take another sip. "Today I have only bad news and more bad news." She paused again and, for the first time, looked directly at Bear.

"You look different," she said and tilted her head, studying her friend. "You get laid or something?"

Bear sighed. She didn't want to lie to Linda, but she didn't want to stop pretending it never happened either.

"There's some good news right there!" Linda enthused, pointing at Bear. "And I want to hear all about it—"

"There's not much—"

"But I've got some other things to tell you first."

"OK," said Bear, relieved.

"Some of the bad news has to do with me, and some of the bad news has to do with you," she said. "Which do you want to hear first?"

"Let me hear what's going on with you."

Linda took another sip of her rum latte, then poured more rum and shook her head.

"I'm going to talk about you first while I finish this off, if you don't mind."

"OK."

"Rick, your landlord, called me," Linda began, her eyes cast down toward the counter. "Said he got a complaint from a concerned neighbor." Bear felt a knot forming in her stomach and wished Linda had brought a bigger bottle. "He said they're concerned that a gang may be targeting his tenant and wanted to know if he had vetted you properly." She took a deep breath and exhaled. "He thinks it would be best if you found another place, Bear Bear. Says they're concerned for their safety."

"OK," said Bear. She felt numb. Truth be told, she hadn't felt comfortable in the pink house since the robbery. She had loved the place, but now it felt like the malevolence behind that attack lingered in every shadow. "How long is he going to give me to find a place?"

"One month," said Linda. "I'm so sorry, Bear Bear."

"It's OK," Bear murmured. "Are you ready to tell me your bad news?"

Linda took another sip from the mug.

"Could I get a sip of that?" Bear asked.

Linda slid the bottle to Bear and pressed her lips together. "So you remember that DNA thing Micki and I did?"

Bear sighed. "You're not going to tell me she's actually an alien, are you?"

"Worse." Linda shook her head.

"What could be worse than that?"

"Bear Bear..." Linda's voice trailed off. She peered straight ahead as if reading words on a tele-prompter she didn't want to say. "Bear Bear, we found out that we're related."

"What?" exclaimed Bear. "Like cousins?" she asked, resisting the obvious joke.

"Nope," said Linda. "We are"—she paused to raise her cup as if to toast—"half sisters."

Bear's mouth hung open, and her eyes widened. "Oh no." This was definitely worse than alien DNA.

"Yep," said Linda, lifting her mug and letting the last drop of rum fall on her tongue. "I've been fuck-ing my sister."

Bear and Linda faced each other across the counter in silence, weighing the gravity of the situa-tion, until Bear felt a wave of giddiness move through her, tickling her ribs, armpits, and elbows. Then laughter erupted from her throat and shot out her nose. Seeing this, Linda's face contorted, and doubling over, she gave way to a string of rhythmic snorts orchestrated by her heaving shoulders.

When Bear had gained her composure, she put a hand on Linda's shoulder.

"I'm really sorry, Linda," she said. "You two seemed really sweet together."

"What's crazy about it," Linda said, leaning over the counter and speaking in a hushed tone, "is sometimes I honestly felt like I was hanging out with my little sister." She emptied the last of the rum into her mug. "Your turn, Bear Bear," she said. "Did you and Sophie get together or what?"

"Why Sophie?" Bear attempted to deflect, but the flush in her face gave her away. "It could have been anyone."

"Nah, nah, nah." Linda waved Bear's words away. "It's been Sophie from the start with you."

"What?"

"Dude!" Linda blurted. "I may not be psychic like Little Miss Turtle Pants, but I have eyes." Bear could tell Linda was feeling the rum.

"Turtle Pants?" she repeated.

"Don't change the subject." Linda pointed, teasing, then lowered her voice. "She does have a weird thing for turtles, though. But seriously, Bear Bear, I'm happy for you guys. You make a really cute, weird couple."

Bear shook her head. "I'm not thinking about us that way."

Linda squinted and waved her finger again. "Hold up," she said. "Sophie's not the hookup kind and you know it."

"What I'm *saying* is," Bear said, punctuating each word, "I *can't* think of us that way."

"Why?" Linda shrugged unsteadily. "Fucking Ronnie?"

"No," Bear sighed. "Catherine."

The next morning held a hint of cool air that signaled the coming winter months, and though the change of seasons in Florida was more subtle, Bear could feel it in the slant of the sun and the scents carried on the breeze. The kitchen door was open to the cool shade of the mango tree and to Anoki's van, which had returned sometime during the night.

The thick aroma of onion and garlic in the pan, which usually soothed Bear with a sense of home, evoked instead a sense of restlessness. She felt impatient with the rosemary and thyme leaves. Despite her best efforts not to, her thoughts returned again and again to the last message Sophie sent yesterday evening, just before her meeting with Catherine at a local restaurant.

No matter what happens, Bear, please know that I hold you close to my heart.

Nothing about Sophie's words gave Bear the kind of assurance she had hoped for. The *No matter what happens* part meant that anything could happen. For Bear, Sophie may just as well have written *That thing you fear the most... yes, that thing you are thinking of right now, the thing you are imagining might happen will most likely happen.* And *I hold you close to my heart* was hardly better. There was a big difference between holding someone close to one's heart and holding them *in* their heart. Bear thought of the love poem by ee cummings, "I Carry Your Heart with Me" and how differently it would have read if he had written *I Carry Your Heart Close to My Heart.*

Or maybe she was just overthinking it. Still, dismissing her over-analysis of Sophie's words gave her little peace.

Bear added a pitcher of coconut milk to the onion and garlic mix, sprinkled in the chopped rosemary and thyme, and slid the diced potato, sliced carrot, and chopped kale off the cutting board into the pot. In today's soup special, creamy potato kale, the magic of rosemary brought together a comforting mix of sweet and savory ingredients.

The quiet of her kitchen was interrupted by loud voices and laughter that flowed through the screen door from the parking lot. Anoki had returned to her spot under the mango tree, and it sounded like she had company. Bear put the soup on simmer, grabbed a pack of smokes, and stepped outside.

Anoki stood by the sliding door of her van, looking like she had slept in her overalls for a week.

"Look who I dragged to Colorado!" she shouted, gesturing to the footboard of her van, where Toni, Debbie the Dominatrix's admirer, sat barefoot, wearing sunglasses impossibly too big for her face, shorts, and the *Edward Scissorhands* T-shirt she had worn the last time Bear had last seen her. The shirt looked as rumpled as Anoki's overalls. She waved and smiled, a freshly lit Black & Mild between her teeth.

Anoki collected trash from the floor of the van and stuffed it into a CVS bag, and Bear brought coffees out to them as they settled on the bench outside the kitchen door.

"So, how did you two end up traveling to Colorado together?" she asked.

Anoki and Toni looked at each other and chuckled.

"Well... so... like, it was bingo night," Anoki began, "and I was sitting out here listening through the screen door."

"Debbie terrifies her." Toni laughed.

"And when the show was over, I was watching everyone leave," continued Anoki, "and then I saw this amazing lady. I just walked up to her and said, 'Hey! You wanna go on an adventure?'"

Bear's eyes grew wide. "That's wildly romantic, Anoki," she said.

"Right?" Toni chimed in.

"And... and... she looked me up and down and went to the kitchen door and asked you if you knew me...."

Bear laughed. "And I told her you were a friend. I remember."

"Yeah! And so she said, 'Hell yeah!' and she got in my van."

"And she drove off." Toni laughed.

"Did you know where you were going?" asked Bear.

"Nope," said Toni. "We got about fifty miles north, and I finally asked."

"And I told her we were going to a gathering in a beautiful national forest," said Anoki.

"Now this is the part when I could have freaked and jumped out of the van," Toni said, "but for some reason, I trusted this crazy woman."

"So we drove all the way to Colorado for a Rainbow Gathering in the Arapaho National Forest."

"A Rainbow Gathering?" asked Bear.

"Picture hundreds of people just like Anoki," said Toni, "camping out in the woods, getting high, and singing 'Kumbaya' around a fire."

Bear laughed. "That does sound like an adventure."

"But here's the freaky thing," Toni continued and took a sip of her coffee. "Rainbow Gatherings are her sperm bank."

Bear looked at Anoki with raised brows and laughed.

Anoki shrugged. "Mostly peaceful, earth-loving guys there," she said. "And, like, I want to make my own little family, you know?"

Bear could see it: Anoki and her little one traveling around in that van, a sweet little vagabond family.

"Finally!" Toni blurted. "I meet a woman more badass than me!"

"And possibly pregnant," Bear chuckled.

Bear sat at the tiny desk in the corner of the kitchen and scrolled through the Craigslist rental listings. She had found two possible rentals and had just jotted down the contact numbers when the bell on the front door chimed.

A round-faced teenage girl stood at the counter. "I was wondering if you are hiring," she said. Her blonde bangs looked like she had cut them herself. She wore a flowered skirt that looked a size too big and was pulled together with a belt. Her red boat shoes matched the skirt's red, petaled flowers. What stood out the most was her green T-shirt, with a lone sea turtle swimming in a whimsical, curlicue current.

"What's your name?" Bear asked.

"Brandi. Sometimes I perform at your open mic nights. I play bass."

That jogged Bear's memory. She usually turned away job seekers—she could barely pay herself, after all—but for some reason, Bear felt she should not be so quick to turn Brandi away. "Could you come back tomorrow for an interview?"

Brandi's face lit up. "Yes! Of course!" she exclaimed.

Bear nodded at the young woman across the counter. Brandi would be a perfect fit for Les Beans Café, and it was high time Bear hired some help, especially for open mic nights and busy lunches. She would have to look at her numbers, though, and figure out how to make this work. Even as Bear watched Brandi hop on her bicycle and ride off, she had a feeling she was looking at her very first employee.

The living room of the pink house was quiet, and the crescent moon rose beneath the stained glass hummingbirds in the window. Bear reclined on the sofa with a cup of tea and thought of Sophie. How she wished she were here, playing something beautiful on the piano, eating cold figs and stuffed olives. Bear closed her eyes and recalled their lovemaking, the tenderness and laughter, the salty taste of Sophie's skin, the warm gush of her river.

The tinny ring from the flip phone on the end table interrupted Bear's thoughts.

"How are you, Bear?" Sophie asked, her voice timid and distracted.

"I was just thinking about you," Bear said softly.

Sophie remained silent for a moment, and Bear's heart tightened.

"I wanted to call you," Sophie began. The words sounded heavy, like sandbags lifted with great effort. Bear held her breath. "I wanted to tell you that I have decided to recommit to Catherine. We're going to try again, Bear."

"I understand," Bear whispered, but it was a lie. She didn't understand at all.

"I'm so sorry, Bear."

Bear sat for a long time with the phone open to dead air. She wondered if Catherine had been in the room, watching Sophie heave her sandbags and not lifting a finger to lighten her load. Bear closed the phone. What did it matter? Sophie was gone.

Bear poured her cold tea into the sink, reached for the opened bottle of red on the counter, and filled her teacup to the top. She stood over the sink and drank half, then refilled the cup. No tea and sympathy tonight, she thought. She would rather drink her self-pity into oblivion.

Chapter 11

The morning sun hung low in the east, casting long shadows across Lakeside Avenue and Bear's path to the café. She had fallen into bed drunk and gotten up with a pounding in her head that blinked reminders of every pitiful thought she had washed down. She took a long drag off her clove cigarette and tried to plan her morning as she walked. She had to call about those rooms for rent on Craigslist; fix the chain on the toilet flusher; change the light bulb over the Les Bean sign; bag, label, and restock the coffee; and wash the basket of Brussels sprouts for the soup of the day. Most of all, she needed to stay busy enough not to think about Sophie's life with Catherine or her own pitiful life without Sophie.

Simon stood in front of Walton's Sports Bar across the street when Bear came around the corner. He held a hose in one hand and a broom in the other.

"Things get a little messy last night, Simon?" she asked, eying the stains on the sidewalk in front of him.

"Pigs!" he blurted, then put down his broom. "Hey, Bear, I gotta ask you something."

"Sure, Simon."

"Ya see, Ronnie usually takes care of me," he began, "but when I saw her this morning, she said she couldn't, so—"

"You saw her this morning?"

"Yeah, yeah," Simon said, waving off the question. "She came by to get a couple things—"

Bear looked across the street to the café door, which stood ajar.

"And I thought she was going to give me that twenty she promised, but—"

"She was supposed to pay you twenty dollars?"

"Yeah, yeah." Simon nodded. "For keepin' an eye out."

Bear nodded slowly and let out a sigh.

"I don't mean to bother you for it, Bear, but I could sure use it." Simon searched her face. He looked hungry and in need of a shot of whisky.

Bear reached into her pocket where she had stuffed a ten-dollar bill.

"I've just got ten on me, Simon."

"'Preciate it, Bear!" Simon stuffed the bill in his front pocket and returned to his broom.

Bear jogged across the street to the open front door and stepped in, her mind racing ahead to her hiding place for the cash. She ran to the kitchen, popped open the lid on a five-gallon bucket marked "Garbanzo Flour," grabbed a pair of tongs, and dug into the flour for the plastic ziplock bag that held close to $1,000. Rent money, coffee and produce money. She pulled the bag free and breathed a sigh of relief. Bear replaced the bag, closed the lid, and looked around again. Everything looked as she had left it the night before. She stepped out into the front room and then into the bathroom.

"Shit."

The wall opposite the sink, where a framed painting of a lady knight and her lover once hung, was bare.

Moments later, Bear scrolled through the names of local locksmiths. It wasn't exactly legal to change the locks on the co-owner of a business, nor was it exactly legal to create a separate corporation with a separate bank account, but these were her next moves. This was survival.

The Brussels sprout bisque, a favorite at Les Beans Café, surprised and delighted customers with its unusual combination of ingredients.

"Raspberries and Brussels sprouts are secret lovers," Bear often quipped. The bisque, a simple puree of Brussels sprouts with onion and garlic, topped with sautéed sweet onion and a drizzle of raspberry sauce, presented a treat for the eye and palate.

Bear had just finished writing down the chalkboard specials and hung it on the wall when she heard a familiar voice coming through the kitchen door. Anoki's boyish grin beamed above Toni's toothy smile through the screen.

"Anything we can do for a cup of coffee?" Anoki asked. "We're kinda broke at the moment."

Bear laughed.

"As a matter of fact, I've got some things you can do." She gave them her list, and Toni delegated.

"You're not getting on a ladder," Toni instructed Anoki. "You could be preggers." Anoki rolled her eyes and took the toilet flusher assignment. Toni grabbed the ladder and headed to the front door just as Brandi walked in.

"Hey, Bear!" Toni shouted. "A little Dutch girl is here!"

"That's Brandi," Bear explained with a good-natured eye roll.

"Brandi!" Toni exclaimed, holding the door open for her. Toni gestured dramatically to show Brandi the way to the front counter, then slid out the door with her ladder in tow.

"That's Toni," Bear said, nodding toward the front window where, on the other side, Toni had clambered up the ladder holding a light bulb. "I hope she hasn't scared you off."

Brandi laughed. "Not at all."

Brandi stayed after her interview and worked though lunch. Bear listened from the kitchen to Brandi's light chatter with customers and chuckled softly to herself at the girl's sweetness. Brandi seemed like a teenage version of Sophie, and some-how, her presence helped ease the pinch in Bear's heart. *Nonna may have had a hand in this, too*, Bear thought.

"Thank you, Nonna," Bear whispered as she rolled out the naan dough and placed it on the grid-dle.

191

"Someone would like to speak to you, Bear," Brandi said from the doorway to the front room. "Do you have a minute to speak to her?"

Bear craned her neck to see who was at the counter.

"Thought I'd stop by and invite you to go fishing later." The woman from the electric company stood at the counter, smiling wide. "I also would love a latte," she added and turned her smile to Brandi.

"So nice to see you..." Bear began and realized she did not know the woman's name.

"Portia."

"Portia. What a great name!" Bear exclaimed.

Portia laughed. "Thank you. It's a pretty fitting name for someone who likes to spend her time by ocean inlets."

Bear laughed. "I was thinking of the heroine in a Shakespeare play."

"That too. So the tide is coming in tonight, and it's a full moon. I'm going to be at my spot, sweet-talking the ocean perch. I've got an extra pole, if you want to come out."

"I'd like that," Bear said. "It's a late night for me, though."

"I'll be out all night. You know where to find me!" Portia turned and nodded toward Brandi and walked through the door with the grace of a watery, mystical being who could move between worlds.

When the lunch rush had subsided, Brandi sat under the mango tree with a bowl of Brussels sprout bisque, a piece of warm naan, and a glass of iced tea. Bear peered through the screen of the kitchen door.

"I wonder where Anoki and Toni went," she said, eying the empty parking space under the tree.

"They said they had some pools to clean," Brandi offered, "but they're coming back for open mic night."

"Are you up for working open mic tonight?" asked Bear.

"I'd love to," Brandi said. Bear chuckled softly. Just like that, her open mic night worries were solved. Brandi looked up from her bowl. "I'd love to watch how you make this someday," she said.

"It's pretty simple." Bear stepped out of the kitchen and reached in her pocket for a clove cigarette. "I can show you how to make all of them, if you want."

Brandi's eyes widened with excitement and made Bear's heart pinch at the memory of her own excitement years ago in Nonna's kitchen.

Micki arrived at seven o'clock for open mic night, seeming uncharacteristically quiet and subdued.

"I'm sorry about the whole DNA thing, Micki," Bear said. "It must have been quite a shock."

Micki nodded. "It's so crazy, Bear." She leaned over the counter. "I'm sad because I lost a really great girlfriend, but I found a sister, you know?" She squinted and tilted her head. "Linda's my *family*, Bear!"

Anoki and Toni reappeared and claimed their spot on the sofa.

"Got cash now, Bear," Toni chimed from the counter, waving a ten-dollar bill. She turned to Brandi. "I'll have a couple of iced coffees with vanilla, Brandi, fine girl."

The open mic crowd poured in, and the performers, most of whom knew Brandi from her own performances, greeted her at the counter with surprise and delight.

"What's a breve latte, Bear?" Brandi asked, poking her head into the kitchen.

"Someone ordered a breve latte?" Bear asked. The only customer who had ever ordered one was Sophie. Bear's heart skipped a beat. She peered around the kitchen door just enough to see who was at the counter.

"Linda!" Bear could not hide her surprise as she moved around the counter to greet her. "I thought Sophie was here." Linda folded her arms around Bear.

"Sophie asked if I would have a breve latte for her," Linda said. She squeezed Bear's shoulders and looked into her eyes. "She sends her love, Bear."

Bear felt tears well up and tried to nod them away, then felt Linda's arms around her neck again.

"Thank you," she whispered. A friend's embrace was exactly what she needed just then.

"Those are some beautiful words you say at the end, Bear." Anoki rested on the sofa after the doors were locked and the tables cleaned. The afterparty had grown to five. Anoki and Toni cuddled on the sofa. Linda had claimed the love seat, which she shared, platonically, with Micki. Bear pulled up a chair.

"Those are the last words my nonna said to me." She touched the silver ring with three stones that she wore around her neck. "This is her ring."

"That's cool." Anoki nodded. "What are the stones?"

Bear held the ring in her fingers and touched each stone. "Turquoise for protection, blue lapis for wisdom, and carnelian for creativity," she said.

"Your nonna sounds pretty special," said Anoki.

195

Bear nodded. "She was... and still is."

"If your nonna was here right now, Bear Bear," Linda said, "what do you think she'd say to you?"

Bear sighed. "I think she'd tell me that there is nothing to fear. No reason to doubt."

"Sounds like a Radiohead song!" Micki piped up.

Linda laughed. "Your nonna has a wide sphere of influence!"

Bear chuckled. Linda had no idea how true her words were, she thought. After all, Nonna probably had something to do with every one of them walking through that front door.

"Do you feel pregnant, Anoki?" Bear asked. "When will you know for sure?"

"Aw, yeah, I feel like I am, for sure," Anoki said, absently holding her hand to her belly.

"She's glowing already!" Toni beamed.

"Have you guys thought about bringing little ones into the world?" Anoki asked and looked around at the other women.

"I'd like to one day," Micki replied.

"Me too," said Linda, "but I want to be the daddy." The women chuckled softly. Their eyes traveled to Bear, who sat, smiling at the inside of her mug.

"What about you, Bear?" asked Anoki. "Have you ever thought about it?"

Bear looked up, still smiling. "Oh, yes, I've thought about it," she said and pressed her lips to conceal her smile, but the women had already noticed.

"Do tell," said Linda.

"I thought about it all the time with Bella," Bear began, then shook her head. "But we only talked about it once." She nodded as if to signal the end of the story.

"And?" Linda pressed.

Bear looked around at the expectant faces of her friends, then relented.

"We were on vacation in Provincetown. I remember how wonderful it was to feel so free with her. We were on a whale watch—standing on the deck of the *Portuguese Princess*—and a mother whale and her calf had come very close to the boat. It was like the momma whale was showing off her beautiful baby—"

Bear was surprised that her voice cracked and tears welled when she recalled the mother whale and calf. Linda nodded her on, and Bear continued with a quavering voice.

"I guess we were both so caught up in the beauty of it. I told her I thought about having a baby with

197

her all the time, and this time Bella didn't flinch. She didn't remind me how impossible that was. She just smiled and played along. She asked if I would want a boy or a girl, and I said I'd be happy with either, but I had dreamed about the two of us walking in the park with a little girl."

Bear paused to steady her voice as the image of that dream rushed back—the golden autumn leaves of Inwood Park scattered along the path, she and Marabella each holding a mittened hand of a little girl, who playfully kicked up the bright leaves between them.

"She asked me if I had dreamt up a name while I was at it, and I told her, as a matter of fact, I had. And this made her laugh, and her laughing about it and not reminding me of the impossibility of it made me feel even happier—maybe bolder too. I told her that I had already named our little girl Esperanza. Now, this made Bella laugh the hardest. At first I thought she was laughing because she had expected me to say a more American name, but she told me that, while Esperanza was a beautiful name, no one called their baby girls that anymore because in the Spanish *novelas* on TV, almost every maid and servant was called Esperanza, and no one wanted their little girl to be named after a maid or servant." Bear shrugged. "I told her I was sticking to Esperanza unless she came up with a better name."

"That's a great story," Linda said. "And sad, in a way."

Bear nodded, relieved that Linda could see the beauty and the sadness in it.

"It's like that little girl you dreamt about was really the dream of your relationship," Linda continued as if thinking out loud. "Full of hope, but impossible."

Bear smiled grimly and thought of Sophie. "That seems to be a pattern with me."

Bear walked along Lakeside under the full moon. Linda had offered her a ride, but Bear didn't want to go home right away. The day had been so full, she felt she had barely enough room for all the thoughts that swam around in the swirling currents of her mind. She missed Sophie, and going home to an empty bed would only make that worse.

At Lake Worth Avenue, Bear turned left toward the bridge. The streets were quiet, and the scent of night-blooming jasmine filled the air.

"How's the fishing?" Bear shouted over the rail toward a figure sitting in a lawn chair below.

Portia looked up and smiled. "Nothing yet!" she shouted. "They must be waiting for you!"

As promised, Portia had an extra pole and plenty of bait shrimp for Bear. A cool breeze flowed along the canal, and the incoming tide was luminous and rippling under the moonlight. Bear cast out and sat down next to Portia with a sigh.

Portia chuckled. "Sounds like you got a busy mind. You came to the right place then." She pointed up. "Full moon for illumination." She pointed at the water flowing past them under the bridge. "Incoming tide bringing in all the answers from Mother Ocean."

"Sometimes, when I'm telling a story about my life," began Bear after a moment, "I realize that my life is mostly a tragedy." She studied the end of her pole and watched its slight movement with the tide. "But all the while I'm telling it, I'm thinking it's a romance or a comedy."

Portia threw her head back and laughed, her voice echoing off the bridge above.

"You sound like every human I know."

Bear sighed, pulled a pack of Djarums from her bag, and lit one.

"I know, right?" Portia said with a chuckle.

"I didn't say anything," Bear said.

"Not talkin' to you, Bear."

Bear looked around. "Who then?"

"That nice ol' lady who's always with you," she said.

Bear scowled. "Are you playing with me right now, Portia?" She had not told Portia about Nonna, had she?

"No, but you could sure use some playtime with *someone*," Portia harrumphed. "You wound up tight."

"What did she say, then?"

"She said she wishes you could see yourself like she does," Portia said.

"How's that?" Bear asked.

Portia let out a laugh. "That's pretty generous of you," she said.

"What?" asked Bear.

"Not talkin' to you, Bear," said Portia.

"Jesus Christ," Bear muttered.

"Not him neither."

"Portia..."

"OK, OK, keep your panties on," Portia said. "I think she's being a bit too generous, 'specially with that mashed-up face you got on right now, but she says you're beautiful and perfect. But like I said, I don't really agree..."

Bear stood up so quickly she knocked over the bucket she was sitting on and tipped over the shrimp cooler. She looked around, toward the street above, across the canal, along the walkway

201

under the bridge, but she could see no shadow, no silhouette, no misty shape. *Why can't I see you?* she asked silently, her question echoing in the darkness of her mind.

"Nonna," she whispered.

But Nonna was gone.

Chapter 12

The small, one-room cottage looked no bigger than a converted shed and was most likely just that. Bear stood in the center of the room and listened to the owner go on about all the cute little things they had done to make it a lovely place for the perfect tenant. The kitchen sink was the size of a bar sink, and cooking had to be done on a two-burner hot plate. The owner, a woman in her fifties, in kelly-green capris and a white Izod jersey, stood smiling and nodding.

"What do you think?" she asked. "I think you would be a perfect fit for this cottage."

Bear had exactly seven days until her moving date, and so far, this was the best option she had seen. Still, she didn't feel enthused about living in a converted shed behind this woman's house.

I love this — its about the seen + trust in the unseen

"Can I let you know by tomorrow?" she asked, though she had no idea how her situation could change in the next twenty-four hours.

She looked forward to the peace of the café kitchen, quiet contemplation, and maybe a chat with Nonna. If all else failed, she could always camp out on the café's sofa for a week or two and shower at the beach. She wouldn't exactly be homeless, but she would be close.

Bear's hopes for finding sanctuary at the café evaporated when she rounded the corner and saw Ronnie's car in the parking lot, then, just beyond the mango tree, a tow truck backing a dumpster into a tenant parking space.

"What's going on?" Ronnie's voice came from the window of her car.

"I have no idea," said Bear, watching the tow truck lower the dumpster into place. She turned to Ronnie. "What's going on with you?"

"I see you've changed the lock." Ronnie stepped out of her car.

"Do you blame me?"

"No." Ronnie smiled. Bear tilted her head. "I've come to talk to you about something."

Bear held up her hand. "Me first," she said. "I want some explanations."

"For what?"

"The bank," Bear said, holding up her thumb and beginning a count. "The complaints about the business, the call to my landlord, paying Simon to spy on me, taking things from the café..."

"OK, OK." Ronnie held her hands up as if she had been stopped by police. "I did freeze the account, but you left me holding the bag with our mortgage. And that art piece was mine, Adelina."

"And the complaints?"

"I had nothing to do with that."

"The call to my landlord?"

"I don't even know where you live," Ronnie said and crossed her arms. "How could I do that?"

Bear sighed and shook her head. "And Simon? Did you pay *him* twenty dollars to spy on me?"

"I wouldn't give that bum a dime."

Bear squinted toward Ronnie and stood like a stone with her arms crossed.

"I've got to open soon," she said finally and turned toward the door.

"Quick question," Ronnie said, stepping closer. "Who's Sophie?"

Bear clicked on the espresso machine behind the counter and moved into the kitchen, ignoring

Ronnie, who had followed her inside and now stood at the counter tapping her fingers.

"Well?" she asked. "Are you going to tell me who she is?"

Bear put her apron on, tied the strings in the back, and turned her gaze to Ronnie.

"You don't get to ask me questions like that anymore, Ronnie." She turned again toward the kitchen.

"Fine," said Ronnie. "That's not what I wanted to talk to you about, anyway."

"I've got a ton of things to do—"

"I think it would be best for both of us if you signed a quit claim on the house," said Ronnie.

"Quit claim?"

"It releases you from the mortgage," Ronnie said. "That's what you want, isn't it?"

Bear stood in the doorway of the kitchen and studied Ronnie's face. The offer sounded exactly like what she would want. She wondered if there was a catch. For the moment, Bear couldn't see a hint of a trap behind Ronnie's eyes. But that didn't mean much.

"I'll think about it," she said.

A few hours later, Bear gathered the ingredients for the soup of the day, black bean chili, and eyed the dumpster in the back of the café through the kitchen window. Brandi had arrived early, though blessedly after Ronnie had gone, and stood over a bowl of assorted dried peppers on the prep table. Bear picked up each pepper.

"These are the chili peppers," she said. "Great heat." She picked up another. "This is chipotle pepper," she said and held it up for Brandi to smell it. "We get a nice, smoky flavor from these." She picked up a dark green pepper. "This is poblano pepper," she said. "A milder pepper, but it adds great flavor!"

"What are you going to do with them?" Brandi asked.

"We're going to roast them in a cast iron skillet," Bear said. "Would you like to do that part?"

Brandi nodded, wide-eyed.

"We have to do this outside," Bear instructed. She gathered the single butane burner and the cast iron skillet and set up Brandi's cook station on the table outside the kitchen door.

"You want to toast them lightly on each side," she said. "This brings out the best in each pepper."

An hour later, the two stood over a large pot of chili.

"What are you doing for Thanksgiving?" Bear asked.

Brandi carefully stirred the pot.

"I have to spend it with my family," she replied, "but I'd rather spend it with my friends." She put a spoonful of chili into a small bowl and added, "I can't wait to move out."

Bear thought about her own senior year in high school, how freedom had come at a high price: the loss of her family. It was a loss she had felt on her graduation day and on every birthday and holiday since.

"Moving out is a big decision," she said. "It affects your life in ways you can't imagine." Bear sprinkled shredded cheddar on her chili. She wanted to say, *If you lose your family now, you'll spend the rest of your life looking for a replacement.* But who was she to advise anyone?

"What are you doing for Thanksgiving, Bear?" Brandi asked as she wiped up the chili on the bottom of her bowl with a piece of naan.

Bear watched the strips of shredded cheddar melt into her chili. She had no idea what she was doing for Thanksgiving. As far as she knew, she was spending it alone.

"Maybe I'll offer a Thanksgiving meal for folks who have nowhere to go," she said.

"That's very kind," Brandi said.

Bear looked up from her bowl. Sometimes Brandi sounded so much like Sophie that Bear caught herself looking for her behind Brandi's face. She smiled faintly. Kind? Or just avoiding how alone she'd be on Thanksgiving, and how much she wished she could spend it with Sophie.

"Well, hello there!" A man's voice came through the screen of the open kitchen door. Bear turned to see her landlord, a thin, red-haired Canadian in his forties, wearing overalls and a dusty T-shirt.

"Hey, there!" Bear exclaimed. "What a surprise to see you!"

"Had to come down a month early this year because the tenant upstairs abandoned her place." He shook his head. "Left me a mess to clean."

"I'm sorry to hear that," said Bear. "What's going in the dumpster?"

"Everything." He laughed.

"You mind if I take a look at the place?" asked Bear. The thought of living above her café felt romantic, even exciting, especially considering her only other option was a converted shed in a retiree's backyard.

"You know someone looking?"

Bear nodded. "I sure do.

Two narrow French doors off the apartment's tiny living room opened to an east-facing balcony that had just enough room for Bear to stand and look to the Atlantic Ocean on the horizon or north and south along Federal Road. She stood on the small balcony and felt her heart quickening.

"I need to level with you," the landlord was saying. "I plan to put the whole building on the market the first of the year. If it's sold, I can't guarantee the new owner will renew anyone's lease."

Bear nodded. "That includes my café?"

"Afraid so," he said.

Bear sighed. Her romantic imaginings of living above her café were slightly dimmed now by a sense of uncertainty. Still, this place would be lovely to live in, even if it turned out to be temporary. "I need to level with you, too," she said. "I'm the one looking for a place to live." She closed the doors to the balcony and looked around at the small, dusty living room. "I'd like to rent this place, if you're OK with that."

He raised a brow and nodded. "That would save me a lot of fuss."

Two weeks later, on November first, Bear stood on the tiny balcony, taking in the view of the street below and the eastern horizon over the Atlantic. Boxes were stacked in a pile next to a bucket of paint in the living room.

"Knock, knock!" a voice shouted from the open door. "Anyone home?"

Linda and Micki stood at the front door, peering into Bear's mostly unpacked apartment.

"Hey, come on in!" she cried. "What a surprise!"

"We knew you might be busy unpacking and all," Linda said, "but we thought you could use a little break."

"We brought a picnic!" Micki sang, raising a stuffed Whole Foods bag in her hand.

Bear arranged three leftover moving boxes for chairs and one box for a table. Linda poured chianti into three paper cups, and Micki opened the plastic deli containers. Olives. Black, green. Garlic-stuffed.

Cheese-stuffed. When Micki pulled a container of figs from the bag, Bear felt a lump in her throat and tears burning the backs of her eyes.

"Sophie told us you love olives and figs," Linda said and leaned toward Bear. "Is this OK?"

Bear wiped a tear and nodded. "How is she?" she asked.

Linda shook her head and sighed heavily. "She's taking it one day at a time, Bear Bear," she said. "Life doesn't come with any guarantees."

Bear nodded, lost in her own thoughts. How foolish she had been to think that Sophie's life would be any more certain than hers. She wondered why, though, Sophie would need to take her days with Catherine one at a time.

"Perilous," she whispered, holding a cool, ripe fig to her lips.

"Things seem kind of quiet with Ronnie these days," Linda said. She had poured the last of the chianti, and their picnic containers were empty. The balcony window had darkened, and a few stars appeared in the east. "Has she finally decided to leave you alone?"

"Maybe," said Bear. "She asked me to sign a quit claim on the house a couple of weeks ago. We have an appointment next week for that."

"Whoa, whoa!" cried Micki. "Hold up a minute."

Bear and Linda looked at Micki, who was shaking her finger. She put her cup down and pointed at Bear. "Do you know what that means?"

"That I'm released from the house?"

"Nope!" Micki exclaimed. "It means that if she sells it, you're released from getting any money, *but* you're *not* released from the mortgage."

Bear had forgotten Micki's business background.

"Technically, you should never sign a quit claim until you've been taken off the mortgage."

Bear frowned. "So you're saying I shouldn't sign it?"

"You need to talk to a lawyer first. I'm going to put you in touch with mine." Micki raised her finger again. "Please don't sign anything until you've talked to him."

Two days before Thanksgiving, Bear sat at the long conference table in the offices of Stein & Barclay and clicked her pen. On the table in front of her, the contract prepared by Micki's lawyer was her passport to a new life, a new beginning. The only thing the contract needed was Ronnie's signature. What had the lawyer called it? *Quid pro quo.*

That's it, she thought. *I'll sign yours if you sign mine.*

The conference room door opened, and Ronnie entered with a tall, slender man in a dark blue suit and pink striped tie.

"Good morning, Ms. Bernardi," the lawyer addressed Bear. "Our notary will join us in a minute. I understand you have a document for my client as well?"

Bear nodded and slid the contract across the table.

"Will you excuse us, please?" The lawyer nodded toward Bear and gestured for Ronnie to step outside with him. Bear sat in silence, clicking her pen again. This was the deciding moment. The contract was simple but covered an entire page of legal language. Ronnie would release all claim to the café, and Bear would release all claim to the house. *Quid pro quo.*

A few moments later a middle-aged man in a slim, blue tie and a white shirt with rolled-up sleeves entered the room.

"Good morning," he said cheerily. "I'm the notary."

Bear nodded, clicking her pen nervously.

The door opened again, and Ronnie returned with her lawyer. Bear held her breath as Ronnie sat across the table, her eyes fixed on the documents.

"So my client has read and understood the contract," the lawyer began. "It is her intention to remove you from the mortgage in as timely a fashion as possible. We understand that this is a concern of yours." The lawyer slid a page of paper across the table. "She has agreed to sign your contract in exchange for your signature on this quit claim deed."

Bear breathed and nodded. She glanced at Ronnie, who still had not looked at her. Instead, she kept her eyes on the documents. Bear clicked her pen one last time and signed on a line marked with a highlighted x. Ronnie quickly signed the contract, pushed her chair out, and left the room. Her lawyer smiled awkwardly and stood.

"We just need to make some copies and you'll be all set, Ms. Bernardi," he said and followed Ronnie out of the conference room.

Bear held the papers tightly as she walked to her car. She was free. Free from that house. Free to start fresh. Les Beans Café was hers, free and clear. She had thought she would feel lighter, but a strange heaviness settled on her shoulders as she drove north on Federal toward the café. With the building going up for sale in a month, this freedom

Patricia Lucia

offered no guarantees for her business. Not a single one.

Anoki and Toni were already parked under the mango tree when Bear opened the café on Thanksgiving morning.

"That's a pretty rough commute these days, huh, Bear?" Anoki shouted out of her van window as Bear came down the stairs from her apartment above the café.

"Happy Thanksgiving, you two."

Anoki hopped out of the van and gestured to Bear. "I want to show you something," she said. She led Bear to the edge of the parking lot and looked up at the mango tree, which towered over the café. "Did this tree have anything to do with you picking this place?"

Bear remembered the afternoon she had jerked the car into the parking lot.

"I think so," she said.

Anoki nodded and pointed to the lush branches above. "See how the branches lean over your café?"

Bear nodded and Anoki pointed to the ground below the tree.

"Which way are the roots growing?" She asked.

"Under the café," Bear said, a new realization growing.

216

Anoki nodded again. "Looks like this place is being held by that tree. Maybe it always has been, you know?" She stopped to light a cigarette. "Whoever guided you here—"

Nonna, thought Bear.

"—seems like it's her way of holding you, too."

Toni jumped out of the van with a lit cigar.

"I don't mean to interrupt all this deep spiritual talk, but we've got some serious celebrating to do too." She handed a fresh cigar to Bear.

"What's this?" Bear asked.

"I told you. We're celebrating." Toni looked toward Anoki, whose cheeks were presently flushed. "We're preggers!"

Bear laughed. "Aren't cigars for celebrating the birth?"

"Nah, nah." Toni waved her hand dismissively. "We're celebrating the whole nine!"

"Are you two sticking around for Thanksgiving dinner?" Bear asked. "I've got enough food to feed the three of you."

"We've got a couple stops," said Anoki, "but we'll come by later."

"And we've got news!" Toni blurted.

"More news than a baby?" Bear asked. Toni and Anoki nodded in sync.

In the kitchen, Bear peeled potatoes while Anoki and Toni leaned on a prep table, Anoki sipping her decaf latte and Toni, her triple-shot espresso.

"Now that we're preggers and all," Toni was saying, "we decided we need to have a real home for the little one."

"So we're looking for a place to rent around here," added Anoki. "I don't even mind if it needs a little work 'cause I can fix anything."

"Yes, you can, baby." Toni leaned into Anoki for a kiss.

"So you're not going to be a little vagabond family?" asked Bear.

"I really like that life," Anoki began, "but we're thinking, like, what's gonna be best for him?"

"Him?" Bear raised her brows.

"I had a dream about him!" Toni said with wide eyes. "We were living in a little house with flower boxes."

"He was already, like, one or two years old, and he was playing with a baby bunny," Anoki said.

"That sounds like a lovely dream." Bear looked up from her cutting board and smiled over the pile of peeled potatoes. They both looked so content, so peaceful.

"Yeah, so we're going to drive around the neighborhood this morning and look for rentals," Anoki said.

"I'd love to be your neighbor." Bear stopped peeling and took in the two of them affectionately.

"You say that now," Toni said over her shoulder as they moved toward the door. "But when we're banging on your door at one o'clock on New Year's Eve, you'll be like, 'Bitches! I'm calling the po-po!'"

Just before noon, Bear lit the Sterno under the food warmers and scanned the table to check if she had forgotten anything. She pulled a double shot and made herself a latte. She was already exhausted and had not even unlocked the front door. She would just close her eyes for a minute or two, she thought, as she settled into the soft cushion of the sofa. Bear's thoughts wandered to Sophie and she wondered if Sophie and Catherine would spend Thanksgiving on the beach with the sea turtles. Bear let out a long, sad sigh. That's how she would have spent Thanksgiving with Sophie.

Bear felt a hollowness in her chest expanding like a sinkhole and the ground beneath her feet giving way to a vast emptiness with no air, no life. She couldn't breathe.

A soft knock on the front window brought her back into the room with a gasp. Simon stood smiling outside the front window. He wore a wrinkled, blue button-down and black trousers without a belt. Bear smiled. Simon had dressed for Thanksgiving dinner.

"You look very handsome, Simon!" Bear said as she opened the door and shook his hand.

Simon's eyes grew wide and round at the sight of the food warmers on the table.

The bell clanged on the front door, and two older women entered, both wearing Christmas sweaters. The shorter woman wore a turkey hat that made her head look like the stuffing. The taller woman, who had bright red hair, clutched a puzzle box.

"Happy Thanksgiving!" The shorter woman nodded and grinned. "Thank you for doing this."

Her taller partner nodded in agreement. "We brought our own after-dinner entertainment." She shook the puzzle box like a rattle.

"Please make yourselves at home and help yourself." Bear gestured to the buffet table, and the women made their way, arm in arm.

The tables filled quickly in twos and threes, and soon the room hosted chatter and light laughter. Bear felt lighter, too, as if the heaviness around her heart had lifted a little, enough to feel grateful for the odd collection of characters occupying her café.

Portia arrived with a sweet potato pie.

"It's a family recipe," she said. "Can't stay, though. Got a date with Mother Ocean."

Anoki and Toni returned just before the end of the day.

"Look who we found!" Toni yelled as they entered under the ringing bell. Behind Anoki and Toni, Linda and Micki peeked in.

"I hope you have room for dessert," Bear said.

"We think we found our place," Anoki announced.

"And we've got stories," Micki said.

"Perfect," said Bear. "I've got pie!"

Hours later, Bear lay her head on the pillow and felt the achy muscles in her back and legs release and relax. Her mind flashed through golden moments from the day. Anoki and Toni's laughter in the kitchen. Simon's smile when she told him he looked handsome. Portia's sweet potato pie and Linda and Micki's funny story about their father—a man neither of them had known, a handsome bass player in a local band, who had sown his seeds in groupie gardens all over Florida.

Bear smiled sleepily and felt a familiar presence. She imagined Nonna sitting on the edge of her bed.

Gratitude will fortify you, Nonna whispered. *Gratitude will light the darkness.*

Nonna's message faded as sleep pulled Bear away, down, down, down into the silence and stillness of a dream.

Bear wandered through a large parking lot that stretched toward the horizon. Someone was playing piano. She followed the sound, searching for the source of such beautiful music.

What a strange place for such beautiful music, she thought.

She came closer and closer to the music, weaving through cars parked erratically before arriving at last at the source, an old black Cadillac where Sophie sat and played a keyboard imbedded in the dashboard, her eyes closed, lost in the melody. Bear wanted to sit with her, but the passenger-side door was locked. She checked the back door; it was locked too.

Sophie continued to play, unaware of Bear's presence until Bear knocked on her door and waved. Sophie stopped playing, her hands frozen above the keyboard and her head turned toward the window where Bear stood. Red tears dripped from her vacant eyes and streaked down her pale cheeks. Panicked, Bear pulled frantically at the locked handle, setting off an alarm. The alarm sounded low and distant at first, then louder.

Bear lay in tossed sheets, sweaty and breathing heavily. The alarm pulled her from the parking lot into her bed, her room and the sound now piercing her sleep. She opened her eyes.

Her phone was ringing. Rolling over, she fumbled for it and squinted into the screen. *2:57 a.m.* Sophie was calling.

"Sophie?" she said, her voice low and froggy with sleep. She cleared her throat and waited for Sophie's response, but heard only silence. "Sophie? Are you OK?"

Sophie's breath shuddered faintly on the other end.

"I don't—I don't want to be here anymore," Sophie whispered.

Bear sat bolt upright. "Where are you?" she asked.

Sophie's breath heaved with muted sobs. "I don't want to be here anymore!" she said again, her voice full of despair.

Bear jumped up and dressed hastily. "Sophie," she said. "Are you home?"

"I don't want to be here anymore," Sophie whimpered. "I don't want to... I don't want to..."

223

"I'm on my way to you right now, Sophie," Bear said as she stumbled into her shoes and grabbed her keys. "You're going to be all right," she continued, hoping to keep Sophie on the line. "It's just that... you're... sad right now, but... you're going to be all right."

The line went silent.

"Sophie?" Bear waited, pressing her ear to the phone and hearing only dead air. "Sophie!"

The Tracer raced north along Federal Road, through dim pools of light beneath streetlamps. Bear's heart thumped faster than its engine, which strained under the weight of her desperate foot.

Chapter 13

Bear pulled up to the curb in front of Sophie's cottage, and her heart sank. Sophie's car was not in the driveway. The kitchen light was on, but Bear could not see through the curtains. She turned the doorknob and was surprised to find it unlocked.

The door scraped loudly over broken glass scattered across the floor. She stepped into the kitchen, and glass crunched under her shoe. A sea of green shards spread across the yellow tile of Sophie's kitchen floor and glistened in a pool of red wine.

Bear glanced toward the stairway to the upper bedroom and froze. Sophie sat barefoot and slumped over, her head buried in her arms, her hands stretched out in front of her as if begging for mercy from a merciless God.

"Sophie," Bear whispered, stepping over the broken glass. But Sophie was silent, motionless, her outstretched hands rigid and still. Bear sat down on the stair next to her and looked closely at her back, which, to her relief, rose and fell with Sophie's breath. She looked down Sophie's outstretched arms to her hands and found a single, pointed shard of glass pressed between Sophie's thumb and finger. Just above the wrist on the other arm a small cut lay open over a tiny pool of red on the yellow tile below. On the other side of Sophie's wrist, a single drop of blood had dried in place, suspended like a raindrop frozen in a winter storm.

"Sophie," Bear whispered again. Tears burned her eyes, and she pressed her lips together against the truth of the scene before her. Steadying her hand, Bear lifted the glass from Sophie's fingers. Sophie remained still, silent, collapsed into herself.

Bear quietly climbed the stairs to the bathroom and gathered a box of bandages, cotton swabs, and peroxide from under the sink. She peered at her face in the mirror, stunned by how pale and frightened she looked. She cleaned and dressed Sophie's cut, then put her hand gently on Sophie's back.

"I'm going to bring you into the other room so you can rest," she whispered. Bear reached under Sophie's legs with one arm and across her back with the other and, willing all her strength, lifted Sophie's limp body from the stair. She descended the two steps into the sunken living room and placed her on the sofa. Sophie grimaced and turned her face away, covering her eyes with both hands. The sight of Sophie like this sent such a pang through Bear's heart that it constricted her throat. She looked around the room, noticing for the first time how it had been ravaged. Books had been knocked off shelves, the piano stool kicked over, sheet music strewn across the floor.

Bear covered Sophie with a blanket and tucked it around her bare feet.

comforting

"I'm going to stay right here, Sophie," she said, keeping her voice as steady as possible. "You can go to sleep." She sat in the chair next to the sofa and listened to Sophie's breathing until it shifted into the quiet cadence of sleep; then she crept back into the kitchen and set about picking up the glass. She washed the wine from the floor and returned to the living room to check on Sophie again. Assured that Sophie was fast asleep, she stepped outside the kitchen door and took out her phone.

"Linda," she whispered. "Something's happened to Sophie."

The sound of her own words, the image of the shattered glass, of Sophie's wrist and brokenness, and her own frightened face in the mirror broke a dam within that had held her own despair at a safe

227

distance. It was now released on a wave of shudder-ing sobs.

Bear sat on a rickety chair outside the kitchen door and pulled a long drag on the clove cigarette that trembled between her fingers. The sun hung low in the morning sky, and storm clouds threat-ened in the west.

"I really appreciate the smokes," she said.

"Thought you might need them," Linda replied, her eyes gazing toward the approaching clouds. They were silent for a long time, Bear fidgeting with her clove cigarette and Linda standing at the edge of the porch, hands deep in her pockets and eyes fixed on a distant thought, forming and twisting into dread.

"So what now?" Bear asked.

Linda smiled grimly. "Now comes the hard part." She moved to the little table and sat down across from Bear. "Can I get one of those?" She reached for the box of Djarums, lit one, and tapped the box on the table. "So I talked to Catherine," she said and took a drag from her cigarette. Bear held her breath. "Turns out Catherine broke it off with Sophie the day before Thanksgiving."

Bear's mouth hung open in disbelief.

"Sophie was alone on Thanksgiving?" she asked.

"Yeah, well, it gets worse," Linda said, exhaling a cloud of blue smoke. "From what Catherine could tell me, Sophie spent Thanksgiving Day on the beach and polished off nearly a whole bottle of wine." Linda took another drag and exhaled. "Then she drove her car over a curb into a street sign and left it there."

Bear put her head into her hands and moaned. "Doesn't she have family close by?"

Linda shook her head. "They may be close by, but Sophie doesn't have any family."

"I don't understand," Bear said, desperation rising in her voice.

"You can't have family if they won't have *you*, Bear Bear."

They fell silent again, the reality of Sophie's unraveling settling uneasily on both of them.

"What are we going to do?" Bear asked. She felt an urgency to do something. Anything.

Linda shook her head. "You're going to open your café this morning and make some amazing soup for your lunch crowd." She smiled and shrugged. "I'm going to take Sophie to the psychiatric emergency care unit."

"But what if she doesn't want to go?" Bear asked.

Linda sighed. "A few hours ago, Sophie didn't want to live, Bear Bear." She tamped her cigarette out and pressed her lips. "Sophie may hate me for what I'm about to do, but sometimes we have to take that risk." She stood up and pushed her hands deep into her pockets again. She squinted past the kitchen door, then back at Bear. "It's best you go now," she said. "You don't want to be around for this."

Bear stared at the pile of yucca on her cutting board, then at the sharp edge of her knife. She laid the knife flat on her wrist and thought of the last words Sophie had said to her. *I don't want to be here anymore.* Bear thought of Sophie in the psychiatric care unit and felt a familiar, prickly feeling crawl up the back of her neck.

A movie scene unfolded in her imagination. In it, she moved stealthily down a hospital hallway, stole scrubs out of a supply closet, and kidnapped Sophie from the psych unit, zigzagging her wheelchair through the crowded hospital corridors with security guards in pursuit. Bear watched the drama play out before her, then closed her eyes and sighed. What a stupid fantasy, she thought. The star, a reckless, deluded hero. Linda had been the real hero today. Bear didn't have the courage.

"Would you like me to cut the yucca, Bear?" Brandi's voice sounded like the voice of someone who had just said, *I'm so sorry for your loss.* Bear looked up from her cutting board and saw that Brandi was holding out a cup. "I made you some tea," she said. Bear nodded mutely. Best she not prepare the soup in this state of mind, anyway.

"I think it took a lot to do what you did last night," Brandi was saying.

Bear held the mug in both hands and frowned into the wisps of steam. She laughed bitterly and shook her head.

"I'm a coward," she said.

The dark clouds that had threatened all morning rolled in from the west, rumbling and cracking against the ocean gusts to the east. A cold rain tapped a warning against the window before it roared down in sheets. Bear felt trapped in the corner of the kitchen, where she sat listening to Brandi chop the yucca, onions, peppers, and tomatoes for the yucca stew. She wanted to pace the parking lot, chain-smoke under the mango tree, and throw her lit butts at passing cars. She wanted to drink a bottle of whisky, then smash it on the ground. She wanted to drunk-dial Sophie and curse her ass out, grab her with both hands and throw her into the stormy waves so she could learn to live again.

231

Bear wiped angry tears from her cheeks, and Brandi looked up from chopping.

"Are you OK?" she asked.

"I just don't understand," said Bear, shaking her head.

Brandi put down the knife and wiped her hands. "I took this mental health class in school, and the unit on suicide gave reasons why people do it." She took a sip of her tea and tapped the side of the mug with her ring finger. "The biggest reason is depression, and another one is, like, this impulse to do it, usually when someone's drunk or high."

Bear nodded. Had Sophie been depressed this whole time? Did she drink too much? She remembered Linda's story about meeting Sophie outside the Bamboo Room. And the night at Sophie's place. Had she missed signs?

"I think it was an impulse thing with Sophie," Brandi was saying.

"How so?"

"She didn't plan it out," Brandi said. "She got really upset and drunk, then tried to cut herself."

Bear nodded.

"Did she feel really ashamed or embarrassed after?" Brandi asked.

"She wouldn't even look at me."

Brandi nodded. "She regretted it," she said. "Try not to get too angry with her, Bear."

Too late, Bear thought.

A sliver of sunshine peeked through the clouds in the west and shimmered on the damp leaves of the mango tree. Bear stood outside the kitchen door, a cigarette in one hand and her phone pressed against her ear in the other. Linda sounded tired.

"How did it go this morning?" Bear asked.

"Rough," Linda said. "But it had to happen. She'll be here for seventy-two hours minimum. It may help her case."

"What case?"

"Her car's been impounded, and her license will probably be suspended for a few months," Linda said. "They found an open container, and she left the scene, so she could get a DUI."

"How does being in the hospital help any of that?" Bear asked, feeling the edges of anger around her words.

"The judge could consider her mental state and be a little lenient." Linda sighed. "For now, she's safe and getting help."

Bear was quiet for a moment and remembered Nonna's words. *Gratitude lights the darkness.*

"Thanks for being the courageous one today," she said. "I couldn't have done it."

Linda laughed. "You're right, Bear Bear. You couldn't. But it's not about courage."

"Isn't it, though?"

"It's because the two of you are so much alike. If this happened to you, do you think Sophie would bring you to the hospital?"

"I can't really imagine her doing that."

"Right?" Linda laughed. "She would feed you soup and chocolate on the couch and have you binge-watch shows about sea turtles."

"That I can see."

"And *that's* why I'm here, Bear Bear!" Linda said. "Someone's gotta save your loopy asses!"

"Got you an early Christmas present," Portia said when Bear approached her fishing spot that evening. She smiled broadly, showing the wide gap in her bright teeth and the deep dimples in her full, dark cheeks. She pointed to a fishing pole leaning against the five-gallon bucket. "I don't use it anymore," she said.

Bear visited Portia weekly now, walking to the bridge after close and sitting beside her with a borrowed pole. She hadn't caught anything yet during her time with Portia, but Portia assured her she was getting closer because the fish had begun to nibble at her bait. According to Portia, this meant Bear was more comfortable with Mother Ocean and the life she held. Bear didn't know about all that, but she did have a new friend in Portia, wise and mysterious, a friend who peered into worlds Bear could not see. Who saw Nonna and talked to her too. The talking part was a mixed blessing. It was one thing to listen to things she didn't want to hear sometimes, quite another when the smiling friend sitting next to her repeated the same message.

"Really?" Bear said. She held the pole and admired the deep, shiny green of the rod and the glint of the guides. Tears welled in her eyes before she could stop them.

"You can*not* be crying over a fishing pole," said Portia, tilting her head and gazing at Bear in disbelief.

Bear dried her eyes with her sleeve and reached into the cooler for a shrimp to cut up for bait. Portia handed Bear her fishing knife and watched as Bear cut the shrimp into smaller pieces and slid a chunk over her hook. She cast out, set her pole on the canal wall, and sat down on the bucket next to Portia's.

"Someone I care about wanted to kill herself last night," Bear said.

Portia nodded, unruffled by even this dire news. "How did you find out?"

"She called me."

"So you talked her out of it."

Bear sighed. "I honestly don't think I helped much."

"She's still alive, isn't she?"

Bear turned to Portia, who gazed back with raised brows, as if to say, *Well?* A flash of Sophie's outstretched arms came back to Bear. The small incision, begun and ended. That single drop of blood, suspended and dried in place above a sea of shattered glass. She thought of her words on the phone. *You're just sad right now, but you're going to be all right.* How pathetic. Was that the best she could do? *You're just sad right now?*

"I didn't say much," Bear said. "Some stupid shit like 'you're just sad right now.'" She lit a clove cigarette and took a long drag.

"Sometimes it's not the words we say," Portia said. She reeled in her line and checked the bait. "It's the sound of our voice that brings someone back. Our voice is our vibrational lighthouse, the Morse code of the soul," she said, resting her pole on the wall. "It's how souls find each other again, and sometimes how they save each other."

The days moved like a holiday parade toward Christmas and the new year. Bear and Brandi hung strings of white lights around the café's front window and a sprig of mistletoe above the front door. Sophie remained in the hospital beyond the seventy-two-hour minimum. Linda assured Bear this was for the best whenever Bear got anxious and twitchy about it.

And still, the parade of days marched on under uncertain skies, to a Christmas without soup making and shot pulling, without smiles and greetings. Bear moved with sighs and cigarettes toward a silent and solitary Christmas.

She found some comfort in making a to-do list for the day. Finish reading that book. Go to the beach. Clean the bathroom. Bring Simon food. And at some point in the afternoon, when she knew her family had gathered in one place, she'd call and wish them all a merry Christmas. She would keep the call brief. Tell them she was out with friends, enjoying the day. They wouldn't ask any questions. They never did.

Bear dreaded Christmas. Every year the same malaise seeped in around Thanksgiving and intensified as the holidays drew near. Before New York and her angel tree Christmases with Bella, Bear had dragged herself home for Christmas, alone. She had learned early not to 'flaunt' her lifestyle if she wanted to come home at all for the holidays, so she came home alone and fueled her holiday spirit with Dewar's and sometimes a clandestine line or two of cocaine with Beth's husband. During her years with Ronnie, Bear's family had made a dramatic turn, fawning over Ronnie like a Christmas doll whenever she brought her home. This had always, and mysteriously, felt worse than the rejection of the past, and it would leave Bear in a subdued state of panic until mid-January, when all traces of the season disappeared. Now she lived where Christmas was celebrated on beaches, where palm trees were decorated with Christmas lights and most Christmas parades floated along coastal waterways. She had thought the tropical sunshine might cure the dread she felt every holiday season, but it hadn't. The sunshine was a buffer, not a cure.

Bear taped a flyer to the café's front window and stepped outside to admire it. The event flyer for Holiday Bingo with Debbie the Dominatrix featured Debbie in a skimpy Santa suit, her whip hoisted in mid-snap, riding a sleigh pulled by women in antlers and little else. Bear sighed. Even this made her sad. It all felt so empty. The holidays. The commercialism. Using sex to sell. *Holy crap*, Bear thought. She had to get out of her head. She should know by now this happened every year.

The phone rang in her apron pocket.

"How you doing, Bear Bear?" Linda asked when she answered. Bear wondered vaguely if Linda had been listening to her thoughts.

"Hanging in there," she said. "Contrary to popular belief, the holidays are not the hap-happiest time of the year."

"I hear you," Linda said. "I've got some pretty interesting news to share, though."

"About Sophie? Was she discharged?"

"Not quite yet," Linda said. "But the good news is—well, I hope it's good news—her parents came to visit her in the hospital."

"Holy shit!"

"Right?" Linda said. "And they've agreed to family therapy."

"That's... that's great, right?" Bear asked.

"It's a step in the right direction, that's for sure," said Linda. "But it's still a long road."

"Will she spend Christmas with her family if she gets out in time?" Bear asked. The thought mostly frightened her. The thought of Sophie with her family, alone and unprotected, made her think of those Christmases in her past, surrounded by family and still so alone.

"That's the plan, Bear Bear," said Linda. "That's the plan."

"Happy holidays, bitches!" Debbie the Dominatrix stood at the microphone, dressed in black faux leather, from corset to city boots, and wearing a red Santa hat. "Have you been naughty?" she asked.

The room erupted into hoots, yelps, and howls.

"How naughty?" she prodded, grinning.

The room was full of familiar faces and some newcomers. Bear hadn't been sure how the Tuesday before Christmas would pan out for an audience, but the café was standing room only.

Linda leaned on the counter in the back and sipped a hazelnut latte spiked with rum. Micki sat at a table with Anoki and Toni, who had arrived early to claim their spot. Brandi weaved back and forth from the counter, carrying drinks, soup, wraps, and Nonna's bread pudding, a recipe Bear liked to break out every holiday season to ease her sadness.

"Come on up," Debbie said and pointed with her whip at a woman on the sofa who had just shouted an affirmation of naughtiness. "Let's hear how naughty you've been, and you'll be punished accordingly."

The woman stepped onto the stage, and Debbie held the microphone to her.

"I threw my girlfriend's cat into the pool," the woman said. The room filled with laughter and hoots.

"There are so many responses to that," Debbie said, peering out into her audience and putting her arm across the woman's shoulder, "all of them containing the words 'wet pussy.'" The room exploded in laughter. "But I'm not going there," she said. "Oh, you're getting your punishment, but I want to get to the root of the problem. Don't you, ladies?" Debbie nodded to the audience. She pushed the woman onto the stool and pointed her whip at her. "Why did you throw the pussy in the pool, bitch?" She held the microphone out and waited for a response.

"The cat was spoiled and obnoxious," the woman said, and when someone booed, she added, "She let it get up on the counters and on the table!"

Shouts and jeering followed.

"So," Debbie began, "you're jealous of a small, furry pussy." The woman smiled and shook her head. "How did this pussy pool party work out for you?"

"She broke up with me."

"Your girlfriend or the cat?"

"Both."

"So the moral of the story is," Debbie said, after the room had quieted, "if you get the wrong pussy wet, no more pussy for you!" She gestured for the woman to stand up, gave her a lash across her hind end, and pushed her back into the audience.

"Remember that, ladies," Debbie said to the raucous audience. "Who can top that?"

Toni stood behind Micki and frantically pointed and gestured toward Micki's head while Anoki attempted to make Toni sit down. Micki sat, oblivious to all of it.

"You!" exclaimed Debbie, pointing her whip at Micki. "Get up here!"

The room exploded in applause, and Micki slowly made her way to the stage, cutting her eyes at Toni, who cheered as if she had just won a prize.

"Your friends think you can top the pussy dunk," Debbie said, drawing Micki closer and tilting the microphone toward her.

"Yeah, but," Micki stammered, "it was an accident." She looked across the room toward the counter, but Linda had disappeared. Bear stood in her place, shrugging and shaking her head.

"I'll be the judge of that," said Debbie. "Now dish it, you naughty bitch."

Cheers and hoots rang out from the audience.

"I started dating this woman...."

"Yes?"

"And I really liked her."

"Yes?"

"I mean I really, really liked her."

"Yes?"

"Then I found out..."

"Bitch, I'm going to whip you if you don't get on with it!" Debbie exclaimed, raising her whip. Toni snorted loudly from the center of the room.

"I found out she's my sister."

The room exploded with gasps of "Oh no!," "What the fuck," and "You gotta be kidding!" One woman shouted, "How was that an accident?"

"All right, all right," Debbie addressed the crowd. "Let's let the very naughty bitch explain herself."

"It's kind of funny, actually," said Micki.

"That's what we're hoping," Debbie said. "So dish it, bitch!"

"I'm adopted, and so I didn't know I had any family," Micki began. "And she said, 'Why don't you do one of those DNA tests?' And I was like, 'I don't know,' so she said, 'I'll do one, too.'"

"That was very sweet of her," said Debbie.

"And then when the results came back, we found out we have the same father."

The room filled with gasps.

"That's quite a story!" Debbie exclaimed. "So you had to break up, right?"

"Yeah, that part was sad."

"Oh, so there's a happy ending?" Debbie asked.

"Sure!" exclaimed Micki. "I have a sister now." She looked around the room again but could not see Linda, who stood listening just inside the kitchen. "She's the best sister anyone could ever have."

The room got quieter.

"Aw," some voices cooed.

"That's sweet," said another.

"And the best part is," Micki continued with more confidence, "I'll have her for life."

The room erupted in applause.

Debbie nodded toward the audience, then turned to Micki. "You're very charming," she said and moved a strand of hair out of her face with her whip. "And you have beautiful eyes. Doesn't she have beautiful eyes?" she asked the audience.

"Thanks," said Micki, grinning. "That's what *she* said."

"That was quite a show," came a familiar voice through the kitchen door.

Bear looked up from the soapy water as her landlord stepped into the kitchen followed by a thin woman in glasses and a dark blue business suit. "Bear, this is Mrs. Pelletier, the representative for a potential buyer."

Bear wiped her hands on her apron and extended a hand to the woman. "Nice to meet you," she said.

"You have a cute place here," said the woman, scanning the kitchen. "Is it exclusive?"

"Pardon?"

"Is this exclusively a lesbian café?"

"No," said Bear. "Not at all."

"The sign gave me that impression," said the woman with a faint smile.

"It's a cheeky pun," said Bear. Something about the woman made it hard to smile back.

"Do you have a lot of entertainment here?" asked Mrs. Pelletier.

"Not much," answered Bear. "Open mic nights on Thursdays, some local singer-songwriters. Debbie's been here a couple of times for bingo night."

Mrs. Pelletier nodded. "Well, thank you for your time," she said and turned for the door. The landlord glanced at Bear and shrugged, then followed Mrs. Pelletier out into the parking lot.

"This tree is unnecessary," Bear overheard her saying. "Taking it down would open more space for parking."

Moments later, Linda peered into the kitchen. "What the hell was that?" she asked.

Micki appeared behind her. "Yeah, who's the suit?"

"Sounds like drama in the kitchen!" Toni yelled from the counter. "Don't start without me!"

"Is the front door locked?" Bear asked.

"I got it!" shouted Anoki.

The five women gathered around the prep table in the kitchen, and Bear locked the back door.

"That," she said, "was the possible new owner of this building."

"What?" Linda exclaimed.

Bear nodded. "The building's up for sale."

"Hope someone else buys it," said Anoki. "She seemed, like... not friendly."

"Les Beans can't go anywhere, Bear!" Toni exclaimed. "We just moved up the block!"

"She wasn't really crazy about that name either," Bear muttered.

"Oh no." Micki looked to Linda for a solution.

"OK, OK," Linda said. "No need to panic. When is your lease up, Bear?"

"May first."

"Then we have time, even if she does buy the building," Linda said.

"That's true," said Micki, nodding. "She has to honor the leases."

Micki's phone dinged loudly, breaking the silence around the table. Micki glanced down at the message and smiled.

"You have such beautiful eyes!" Toni said in her best imitation of Debbie.

"You're so charming!" added Anoki.

Linda rolled her eyes. "I'm going to throw your pussy in the pool!" she blurted.

Les Beans Café closed early on Christmas Eve. After cleaning the prep tables, washing the floor, and emptying the trash, Bear and Brandi sat under the mango tree with a cup of tea each. The streets were quiet, and the clouds in the west glowed pink and gold through the leaves above them.

"I have a gift for you, Bear," Brandi said, putting down her tea and handing her a small package wrapped in green tissue paper. "I didn't have any wrapping paper."

Bear laughed. "I'm not a fan of the stuff," she said. "But I have a little something for you too." She disappeared into the kitchen and returned with a small, cloth-covered journal. "Your gift isn't wrapped at all."

Bear unwrapped the tissue paper and pulled out a T-shirt. A progression of sea turtles swam across the front. Bear laid the shirt on her lap and traced the path of the turtles with her finger.

"I know how much you liked mine," Brandi was saying. "Do you like it?"

A single tear fell from Bear's eye onto the littlest turtle, leaving a dark blot above its fin like a period.

Brandi's eyes widened with worry. "Oh no," she murmured. "I could take it back and get—"

"No," said Bear. "It's perfect." She folded the shirt tenderly and placed it on the table next to her tea. "I never told you why I loved that shirt," she said, wiping her cheeks.

"Sophie?" Brandi asked.

Bear nodded. "You remind me so much of her." She picked up the journal. "For you."

Brandi opened the journal and read the inscription.

"Oh, Bear," she said. "That's beautiful." She turned the pages and found them full of neat print.

"Your recipes!" she exclaimed, but then her expression changed to concern.   "Aren't these supposed to be secret?"

Bear smiled again. "Not to family."

Chapter 14

When the sun rose just after seven o'clock on New Year's Day, Bear had already risen and lit candles and incense in her tiny living room. She had gone to sleep long before midnight, clutching a copy of *The Valkyries* by Paulo Coelho to her chest. A cool ocean breeze floated through the French doors of the balcony and danced with the curls of incense. David Gray sang "This Year's Love" from a mix CD, and Bear found herself singing the chorus and shaking her finger at an invisible audience in the ceiling. Nonna, God, her guardian angels. All of them, she thought. Every last one of them.

She took a sip of her coffee and placed the mug on the top of the bookshelf between Nonna's picture and a solitary Christmas card. On the cover of the card, a whimsical scene unfolded under a full moon and stars, and a sea turtle in a Santa hat carried colorfully wrapped gifts on its back. The card had arrived two days after Christmas and had no return address. Bear pondered the reason for such an omission for days and could only conclude the most obvious reason, a reason that pinched her heart: Sophie didn't want her to write back.

Maybe it was time to let go, she thought. Move on. Find new love. It was the new year after all, and 2009 was going to be a great! Bear flopped on the sofa with her coffee and the Christmas card and sighed. She wondered if she would ever let go.

"Dammit, Sophie," she said out loud.

Sophie had written the date, December 25, 2008, on the top of the inside cover. Bear imagined Sophie sitting somewhere quiet, writing the words Bear read over and over. She wondered if Sophie had sensed how much she had thought about her on Christmas, when she sat out on her balcony and watched the sunrise, when she walked to the beach and along the quiet streets in town, when she stopped at the Chevron station to buy a pack of Djarums and sat under the mango tree to have a smoke. Sophie had filled the silence of Bear's Christmas with beautiful chords, as sad and wistful as the moonlight of Debussy.

Bear shifted on the sofa and placed the card on her heart. She imagined Sophie sitting at the dinner table in her parents' home on Christmas. She wondered if they had been kind to her. Did they recognize the wonder that was Sophie?

Sophie was golden.

Bear recalled a sacred temple in India she had read about, built by so many people who had no gold themselves, but gathered and carried enough of it to cover the walls of the temple because nothing was more valuable, more precious than this sacred place.

Could Sophie's family see that in her?

Bear's thoughts drifted sleepily to a faraway, dusty land, where she walked with a throng of people. She looked across a pool of water to magnificent, golden domes and sat on the cool marble with her bare feet in a long trough of water. Prayer songs floated above her with the mesmerizing notes of a harmonium and lone sitar.

Crack!

Bear jumped out of her dream and looked around, startled. Nonna's picture had fallen from the bookshelf and rested on the floor in front of the sofa. Nonna smiled up at her.

Bear exhaled loudly and picked up her grandmother's picture with unsteady hands.

"If you have something to tell me, Nonna, I wish you would say it without giving me a heart attack."

Patricia Lucia

She curled on the sofa again and returned to the pages of *The Valkyries*. How crazy, she thought, to almost die in the desert looking for one's guardian angel. She glanced at the ceiling.

"I'm not doing that for you," she muttered and went back to the plight of the two characters who were, at this point in the story, vomiting their way back to the living.

"Bear!" a familiar voice called from the street.

"Come out, come out, wherever you are," sang another familiar voice.

Bear moved to the open window and stepped out onto the small balcony. She looked over the railing to the sidewalk, where Anoki and Toni stood waving.

"Hey!" Bear shouted. "Happy New Year!"

"Happy New Year!" they chorused.

"We have something we want to share with you," Toni said. "Can we come up?"

"Sure!" Bear said. "Come around the back."

As Bear made tea for the two of them, she noticed Anoki's baby bump under her sweatshirt.

"How are you feeling, Anoki?" she asked.

"I throw up a lot," she replied with a shrug, "but besides that I feel awesome."

254

"And our place is really coming along," Toni chimed in. "We're fixing it up real nice."

She turned toward Bear, then to Anoki. "We wanted to share something with you."

Bear smiled. "Please do!"

Toni looked at Anoki again and, beaming, pulled out a small, black-and-white, glossy photo. "This is our baby boy at fifteen weeks!"

"Baby boy?" Bear asked, looking up from the photo.

"We're pretty sure it's a boy," Anoki said. "And the technician, she thought so too."

"Aw, congratulations, you two," Bear said. Her eyes moved to Toni's arm resting on Anoki's shoulder, tenderly, almost protectively; then to Anoki's hand on Toni's knee, the other resting gently on her belly. Toni seemed more relaxed than Bear had ever seen her. Anoki's bright green eyes were much brighter than Bear had noticed before, and her hands were uncharacteristically clean.

They're in love, Bear thought, *and they're making a little family.*

"You two look so happy." She felt her heart swell with a certain familiar warmth, as if her own little Esperanza nestled on her lap. "I am so happy for you."

255

"It's going to be a great year, Bear," said Anoki. "You'll see."

"New beginnings!" Toni exclaimed.

"I was just thinking that this morning," Bear said.

"And babies bring blessings," said Anoki, moving her hand across her belly. "For everyone around them."

In the background, Colin Hay sang "I Just Don't Think I'll Ever Get Over You."

Bear nodded. She wanted very much to believe that.

Early Monday morning, the clouds bloomed in towering, pink plumes over the Atlantic, and giant cloud animals formed, moved, and danced. From her balcony, Bear watched a whale cloud and its calf float by; she lit a clove cigarette and sat down on the windowsill with a fresh cup of coffee. A cone of nag champa burned at her feet. She thought of Sophie's card and her heartfelt words of gratitude for Bear's presence in her dark hour, but something Sophie had written echoed in Bear's mind. A kind of warning.

Your café is a beautiful dream, Bear, she had written. *Please, don't become a slave to it.*

Had she?

A bicycle bell rang on the sidewalk beneath her, and a helmeted figure flew by, moving south along Federal Road. She must be a sight to passersby, Bear thought, sitting on her tiny balcony, sipping coffee and burning incense above the intersection of Federal Road and Second Avenue.

She had stepped back into the living room and closed the balcony doors when her phone chimed from the nightstand in the bedroom.

I enjoyed the incense, the message read. *Thank you.*

Bear smiled. Sophie. Of course. Now that she was out of the hospital, she was riding her bike to work. Bear's heart skipped. Sophie would pass her balcony every morning. Every morning, a glimpse, a wave, a shout hello. She might even stop one day under the balcony. An idea formed and sent Bear searching in the closet. If Sophie stopped, she wanted to be ready.

"Mm, cumin!" Brandi said as she entered the kitchen. "What's the soup today?"

"Creamy French lentil," said Bear. "I'm cooking the cumin seeds with the onion and garlic." She stirred the onion, garlic, and cumin seeds in the pan, then added curry powder.

"Can I try making it, Bear?" asked Brandi.

Bear looked up from the pan and smiled. "Sure. Do you have your recipe book?"

Brandi took the journal out of her apron pocket and waved it in the air.

"It's all yours, my dear." Bear handed Brandi the wooden spoon and lingered by the prep table for a moment as the girl gathered the other ingredients. "I guess I'll step out for a smoke, then," she said.

"Sure, Bear," Brandi said. "I've got this."

Bear grinned at her own awkwardness as she stepped out of the kitchen and sat under the tree. She hardly knew what to do with herself if she wasn't working on something inside the café. She remembered Sophie's warning and wondered, Had she become a slave to her dream?

"You know, they're banning those things this year!" someone shouted from the parking lot. She looked up and saw Linda walking from her car, wearing pink candy-cane scrubs.

"What?" Bear asked.

"That's right, Bear Bear," said Linda, grinning. She sat at the table and pointed at Bear's cigarette. "Soon your smokes will be as illegal as mine!" She threw her head back and laughed at the concerned look blooming on Bear's face. "I hate to break it to you, but they're about to ban the shit out of those."

"Why?" Bear asked. "Is this a joke?"

Linda laughed. "Something about flavored ciga-rettes being a danger to kids. Better stock up!"

"Son of a bitch!"

"Or you could switch to my brand."

"I just might," Bear mumbled. This was not a good time to quit, she thought. "Hey, aren't you supposed to be at work?"

"They've got me on nights now," Linda said. "So you get to see *my* smiling smart-ass in the morning."

"I saw someone else this morning, too," Bear said, grinning.

"You trying to make me jealous?"

"I didn't see her face, though," Bear said. "Just the back of her head." She looked up into the tree. "I mean, helmet. I saw the back of her helmet." Bear looked at Linda, who peered back at her through squinted eyes.

"Are you sure you haven't already switched to my brand, Bear Bear? What the hell are you talking about?"

"I saw Sophie this morning," she finally ex-plained.

"Really?" Linda said, sitting up. "Where?"

"She rode by on her bicycle," said Bear. "I didn't really see her, though."

"How do you know it was her, then?" Linda asked.

"Because she thanked me for the incense."

"She thanked you for the incense..."

"I was burning it, and she must have smelled it when she went by."

Linda squinted at Bear again and shook her head, a slight grin formed along the edges of her mouth.

"God, you guys are weird," she said.

Early mornings sparkled now with the flicker of a passing bicycle light and the whimsical sound of its bell. Bear kept her thoughts occupied during the day with recipes and customers and the tidbits of local news they shared over lattes, but nighttime was full of worried thoughts that seemed to hide under the covers, then come out to crowd her pillow with whispers. One sleepless night, Bear sat in bed and opened her laptop, looking for a distraction.

The email was short and to the point, and even though Bear had held her breath while she read the words, it took only seconds to confirm her fears. The building had been sold to the Pelletier Group. All further communications would come from them. She closed her Dell with a snap, placed it on the pillow next to her, and tried to fight the sinking feeling in her gut.

She looked at the clock by her bed. Almost midnight. Her breath became shallow, and that familiar, prickly sensation on the back of her scalp pushed her out of bed and into the living room. She stood still in the middle of the room, listening to her quickening breath, tracking the thoughts that had begun to swirl. Bear felt, as she usually did when panic seeped in, the urgent need to escape it. If she just kept moving, the panic might give up and let go.

She returned to the bedroom and took the clothes she had worn all day out of the laundry basket and put them on. She grabbed a pack of cloves and keys and headed for the door. She needed to walk. She needed to think. Most of all, Bear needed to shake the overwhelming feeling of being utterly alone and out of control, a kind of terror that twisted around her ribs and constricted her breath.

Three blocks south Bear turned east on Lake Avenue and walked toward the bridge. If Portia wasn't there, she'd keep walking to the beach. She stopped to light a clove, her trembling hand shielding the flame. She took a deep breath and tried to slow her thoughts, but a terrifying floating sensation now accompanied them and reminded her of those nights she could not escape her own panic after the Towers came down.

She had nobody, and she had no home. She didn't belong here. She didn't belong anywhere. She had no home. No home. No roots. She could float away. Just disappear. She didn't belong anywhere.

"Portia?" Bear leaned over the rail and shouted toward a shadow below. Her voice sounded foreign to her own ears, and she couldn't catch her breath.

"Bear?"

"Yeah!"

"Why you sound like that?"

"Like what?"

"Like you're fucked-up. Are you fucked-up?"

"Yeah," said Bear. "I'm kinda fucked-up in the head right now."

"Well, get your ass down here. I had a feeling you'd show."

Bear walked along the bridge to where she could climb over the rail to the grass and get to where Portia reclined on a lawn chair. She felt relieved and almost silly for having sounded so freaked out.

"What's going on, Bear?" Portia asked. "Pull up a bucket."

"Just feeling a little crazy."

Portia nodded. "Hmm."

"The building was sold, and the new owners..." She looked toward the water and grimaced.

Portia nodded again, understanding. "Uh-huh."

"And I'm crazy about this woman who doesn't... who isn't..."

"Mm."

"And... and... I feel... lost."

"We're never lost, Bear. Sometimes we take the long way, but we're never lost."

"I don't know where my home is—"

"You've been looking for home for a long time, Bear. You've been looking for home since you left it."

Bear was silent.

"Why don't you talk to your nonna?"

"I do, sometimes."

"*She* doesn't think so," Portia said. "And, man! She's got some shit to say to you!"

"I guess I was avoiding something."

"Well, just because you're avoiding something doesn't make it a good idea to avoid everything," Portia said. "*She* said that, by the way."

Bear sighed.

"She says, 'Ticktock, ticktock,'" Portia said. "Change is coming, and you're running out of time."

"What change?" asked Bear.

Portia grunted and laughed at something Bear couldn't hear. "Right?"

"What?" asked Bear.

"That wasn't for you," explained Portia. "I was agreeing with her. She says you know what's coming. That's why the panic came on tonight. She says your dreams hold the answers."

"To what?" asked Bear.

"Home. Family," said Portia. "They're waiting for you."

Bear scowled. "Am I going to die?"

Portia laughed loudly, her voice echoing off the walls of the bridge.

"Right?" She giggled, then looked at Bear. "Nonna has a great sense of humor, Bear."

"What did she say?"

"She said, 'Eventually.'"

The six a.m. alarm sounded louder than usual. Bear fumbled for the snooze button and flopped back on her pillow. Her mind returned to the bridge and to Portia—and to the reason she had left her bed in the middle of the night in the first place.

She made her coffee and eyed the empty basket on the counter. For two weeks she had carefully filled the basket with things she imagined Sophie might want on a long bicycle ride to work. A cup of coffee with cream and vanilla syrup, ice water, a cup of ice, a dry hand towel, and a wet facecloth rubbed with sandalwood soap. She had imagined lowering the basket to her from the balcony, but that hadn't happened. Sophie had been friendly enough when she passed, ringing her bell and waving, but she had not stopped. Still, Bear placed the usual comforts in the basket and carried it to the front balcony, posting herself in her usual place with her morning coffee and incense burning by her foot.

The sky to the east was brilliant with pink, towering clouds against a turquoise sky. Bear faced north and looked for the small, blinking light of Sophie's bike in the distance.

Today, when Sophie approached, then disappeared under the balcony with a wave and ringing of her bell, Bear turned, as usual, to watch her travel south and out of sight.

But today, Sophie did not reappear on the other side of the balcony. She had stopped.

"Hey!" she called down.

"Hey," Sophie said, unhooking her helmet strap and looking up at Bear through dark sunglasses. "I have just a few minutes."

Bear nodded. "I have something for you." She looked at the basket behind her. Suddenly, she felt embarrassed. "It's a little silly," she said.

"I love silly," Sophie said, removing her sunglasses and squinting up toward the balcony.

Bear held the basket over the rail and gently lowered it, releasing the rope a little bit at a time. She heard Sophie laugh.

"I told you it was silly," she said.

"Oh my!" Sophie exclaimed. She steadied the basket in front of her and looked inside.

Bear tied the other end of the rope to the rail and rattled off the contents.

Sophie found the coffee first and took a sip, then rubbed an ice cube on the back of her neck.

"It's perfect," she said, looking up and smiling. "Thank you."

Bear nodded. There were so many things she wanted to say to Sophie, but she was mute.

"How are you, Bear?" Sophie's question interrupted her stream of thought. "How is your heart?"

Bear pressed her lips together. She felt a sting in her throat and swallowed it.

"Well," she began, looking away from Sophie and toward the east, where the sun cast shafts of light through the clouds. "Sometimes it hurts, and sometimes it's happy. Sometimes I'm scared and lost." She looked down. Sophie had not taken her eyes from Bear, but her smile was gone.

"Remember your name, Bear," she said. "Remember who you are." She fastened her helmet strap again and put on her sunglasses.

Bear nodded and pulled the basket up, feeling awkward and childish about having lowered it in the first place.

Sophie flipped up her kickstand, looked up, and smiled. "Thank you for making this journey beautiful." She rang her bell and was gone.

Ali Stein burst through the door, dressed in a winter coat and gloves.

"It's colder than a witch's tit out there!"

The cold snap had arrived the same day as her performance, and temperatures dipped close to freezing.

"It's nice and cozy in here, though," she said, approaching the counter. "Must be all the Les Beans love and soup."

Bear and Brandi laughed behind the counter.

"Must be!" said Brandi.

Ali winked at Bear. "I bet your bed never gets cold, Bear."

"You'd be surprised."

"I'd be appalled!" corrected Ali. "You *must* have a girlfriend."

"Not exactly."

"That's vague," Ali said.

"That's my love life in a nutshell," replied Bear. "Vague."

"Maybe we can do something about that tonight."

"I don't... really..." Bear began, then backed away toward the kitchen.

"No, no, no," interrupted Ali. "No cold bed for you tonight, Momma."

Brandi snickered. Bear smiled and disappeared into the kitchen.

"What a lovely crowd tonight," Ali said from the stage. She smiled and scanned the crowded room. "Y'all aren't afraid of the cold, are you?" Hoots and cheers rang out. Ali was halfway through her set, and the crowd was warmed up and full of banter.

Micki came to the counter and leaned toward Brandi to order a latte over the noise.

"Are you here with Debbie tonight?" asked Bear.

Micki nodded and smiled wide.

"I didn't see her," said Bear, looking around the room.

"She's right there," Micki said, pointing to a table in the back, where Debbie sat in a faded pair of jeans, ski sweater, and white turtleneck. "She looks different without her makeup and costume, doesn't she?"

Bear caught Debbie's eye and waved. "I had no idea that was her," she said. "How is it going with you two?"

"Wonderful," Micki gushed. "*She's* wonderful."

Bear raised her eyebrows. "So she's not scary in real life?"

Micki shook her head. "That's just an act, Bear," she said. "In real life, she's amazing."

"I'm happy for you, Micki." Bear leaned closer. "How's Linda with all this?"

Micki laughed again. "Like a protective older sister," she said. "And you know what, Bear? I'm going to be the same way with her." She shook her head. "I'm not going to let her settle for bronze or silver when she deserves gold!"

Bear nodded and smiled. She couldn't have agreed more.

"This next song is dedicated to the owner of this fine establishment," Ali said and played a few introductory chords. "Bear is such a sexy name, isn't it?" She grinned toward the counter. Bear smiled at the women who turned around, then squinted a warning at Ali. "And this song is for all of you who braved the cold to be here tonight. I want to make love with every one of you." She ran her fingers across the keyboard with a flourish. "This song is called 'Fuck All Night.'"

Bear and Brandi had just finished cashing out, cleaning tables, and sweeping the floors. Brandi pulled the trash bag from the can in the kitchen and looked up at Bear with a frown.

"I noticed something strange tonight," she said.

"Really?"

"There was this one person who didn't buy anything."

"Huh," Bear said. "That's strange."

"At first I thought maybe someone was buying for her, but she was alone. And there was something else, too," said Brandi.

Bear stopped mopping and looked up.

"She never smiled," said Brandi. "She didn't even look like she was having a good time. Isn't that weird?"

Bear's mind raced. "What did she look like?"

"Middle-aged, I guess," said Brandi. "She was wearing jeans and a baseball cap. Glasses too."

Bear held her breath. "Wire-rimmed glasses?" Her hands tightened on the mop handle.

"Yes!" exclaimed Brandi. "Do you know her?"

Bear nodded. "That was Mrs. Pelletier."

Chapter 15

Bear walked down the narrow alley between Second Avenue and Lucerne to the bank, carrying the money order for February's rent. The letter from the Pelletier Group had given all tenants detailed instructions for paying rent and a list of new guidelines for the property. Tenants were personally responsible for adhering to these guidelines, and businesses were responsible for the behavior of their customers.

She wasn't surprised to see *No drugs or alcohol shall be consumed in public-facing areas*, though she thought of Linda and Anoki enjoying a pipe under the mango tree. What surprised her was the rule against bare feet. *Walking barefoot is not allowed in any public-facing areas.* She thought of Anoki and all the other customers who came from the beach, sandy and barefoot. Was she supposed to police their behavior now? The bold-printed line on the

Patricia Lucia

bottom of the guidelines read *Failure to comply with these guidelines may result in the refusal of the Pelletier Group to renew your lease.*

She stepped out of the bank and lit a clove cigarette. *Guess these will be illegal soon, too,* she thought and exhaled a blue cloud.

"Bear!" a voice echoed from across the street. Portia waved from the sidewalk under the huge ficus tree outside Lake Worth Utilities. Bear darted across the street to greet her.

"Portia!" she said. "You just going to work?"

"Yeah." Portia adjusted the shoulder strap of her insulated lunch container. "How you doing?"

"Trying not to panic," said Bear with a weak smile. "I have a bad feeling about this Pelletier Group."

Portia's laugh surprised Bear. "What's the worst that could happen?"

"I lose my café and my apartment, and I'm jobless and homeless," Bear said, shrugging.

Portia tilted her head. "Are you sure that's the worst that could happen?"

"I'm pretty sure that's the worst thing."

Portia shook her head. "Sometimes we gotta get the worst things out of the way," she said, "before the best things can get to us."

Bear sighed. "Sometimes, I don't understand a word you're saying."

Portia laughed again. "You need to talk to your nonna. Or at least listen when she's talking to you."

"I heard there's another cold snap coming," Brandi said without looking up from the pan. She stirred the spices for Indian-style tomato soup, moving the wooden spoon through cinnamon sticks, bay leaves, cumin seed, peppercorns, mustard seed, and cloves. Bear chopped the onion and garlic and diced the tomato on the other side of the prep table.

"Portia said thousands of snook could freeze to death in this cold snap." Bear held her knife still above the onion, as if she had just remembered something. She thought of Simon under the stairs and hoped he had another place to stay.

Brandi nodded. "I like Portia," she said, without looking up from the pan.

Bear glanced at Brandi, who was stirring with great concentration, and remembered Sophie holding up a dollop of sauce for her to taste. The smallest things reminded her of Sophie.

"I haven't told you about a conversation I had with Portia a few weeks ago," Bear said.

Brandi turned around. "An upsetting conversation?"

"Not exactly," said Bear. "More like a freaky, otherworldly conversation."

"Oh, I love that!" Brandi said.

Bear described the night she had had a panic attack and walked to the bridge to look for Portia. She recalled the strange things Portia had said and admitted she still did not understand what much of it meant.

Brandi leaned back on the prep table with her arms folded, listening intently. When Bear finished her story, Brandi nodded.

"Portia has always felt like an angel to me," she said. "And I'm not surprised she talks to Nonna."

Bear shook her head. "My dreams hold the answers?" she said, repeating Portia's words. "My family waits for me?" Bear chuckled bitterly. "Trust me, Brandi." She returned to slicing tomatoes. "My family up north is hardly waiting for me."

"Maybe it's a future family," said Brandi. "Like Anoki and Toni." She gently lifted the bay leaves, cinnamon sticks, and cloves from the pan and placed them on a plate.

Bear handed her a bowl of chopped onion and garlic, and Brandi emptied it into the pan, stirring the spices, onion, and garlic together.

"Every time I think of my future," Bear said, "all I see is open ocean with no land in sight, like I'm lost at sea."

At one a.m. on Saturday night, Bear stood outside her bedroom, wrapped in two blankets, squinting at the thermostat. She was too cold to sleep. The temperature inside had dropped to sixty-three degrees. Thermostats were still a mystery to Bear, especially when it came to heat. In New York she had never had to turn on the heat in winter. It was always on. If her apartment got too hot, which happened regularly, she opened the window. And it had never gotten this cold when she lived in Boca. She pressed several buttons—once, then again, until she found her way to the heat, then stood, listening for it to click on.

The sudden ring of her phone broke the silence and startled Bear. The name on the caller ID sent a wave of panic rushing through her.

"Sophie?" she answered in a hushed voice. "Are you OK?"

"Did I wake you?"

"No," said Bear. "I'm too cold to sleep." She heard Sophie's soft laugh and exhaled.

"Me too," said Sophie.

"I just figured out how to turn on the heat, though."

"I think it's a button," said Sophie. "With the word 'heat' on it."

Bear laughed. "Well, it's been a long time since I've had to find it."

Sophie laughed again. "I've missed your voice," she said.

"I've missed you," Bear said. She wanted to say, *I've missed everything. Your face, your hair, your scent...*

"There is no heat button in my apartment," Sophie was saying. "I'm wearing so many layers, I look like a snowman, scarf and all." She suppressed another laugh.

"I'm so wrapped in blankets, I look like a tee-pee."

This time Sophie laughed out loud. "I can picture that," she whispered. Then after a moment, she added, "I wanted to ask you if you would talk me to sleep."

Bear smiled. "Of course," she said. "What would you like me to talk about?"

"Anything," said Sophie. "I just want to hear your voice."

Bear thought for a moment. "Well, I hired a young woman to help out during the busy times. Her name is Brandi. Brandi reminds me so much of you that sometimes when she says something I've got to take a second look just to check."

Bear listened to Sophie's quiet chuckle.

"And do you remember meeting Anoki?"

"That wonderfully undomesticated woman who lives in her van?"

"Yes." Bear chuckled at Sophie's description. "She was living in her van for a while, and sometimes she parked under the mango tree. So one night she came to a show at the café and saw Toni. Now, Toni is about the wildest young woman I've ever met. A different kind of wild than Anoki. Well, after the show, Anoki goes right up to Toni and says, 'Hey, you wanna go on an adventure?' Just like that. And Toni looks Anoki up and down, then shouts into the kitchen door, 'Hey, Bear, you know this woman living in her van?,' and when I called back and said, 'Yeah, that's Anoki. She's a friend,' she turned back to Anoki and said, 'Hell yeah, I'll go on an adventure with you.' So Toni climbs into Anoki's van, and they drive all the way to Colorado to this Rainbow Gathering in some state forest up there. And by the time they get back to Lake Worth, these two women are crazy in love and Anoki's pregnant. The pregnancy part of the story I'll have to explain another time."

Sophie chuckled softly.

"But now they're on a motherhood adventure together," Bear continued. "They moved into a little cottage just up the street from the café."

Bear stopped and listened to Sophie's breathing.

"That's a wonderful story," Sophie whispered sleepily.

"And there is this fisherwoman I met," continued Bear. "She works in the utilities building, and she fishes under the bridge. One day she invited me to come sit with her, and she started telling me about the ocean. She says that Mother Ocean has all the answers to every question. That's why she fishes the incoming tide. She's a real mystical kind of woman, and I don't always understand what she's trying to tell me. The other night she started telling me all these things that Nonna has been trying to tell me."

"What did Nonna say?" asked Sophie. She sounded half asleep.

"She said my dreams hold the answers, and she said my family is waiting for me... and that some kind of change is coming."

"Yes," Sophie whispered, almost imperceptibly.

Bear waited for Sophie to say more, but she didn't.

"You know what she meant, Sophie?" Bear asked and listened to Sophie's breathing. She lay wrapped in a cocoon of blankets and listened to Sophie sleep. She held the phone and Sophie's breath to her ear long after her own eyes had grown too heavy and her thoughts had slipped into dreams.

February was such a busy month for Les Beans Café that the days flew by in a blur of bustling lunchtimes. Bear arrived earlier to prep in the kitchen and stayed later most evenings. Open mic nights were more packed as the regular performers drew bigger audiences of fans, and Micki sold more coffee on Thursday nights than Bear did all week.

Sophie had gotten her car back and no longer made the trek to work by bicycle. Sometime in the middle of the month Portia had given Bear a riddle to solve and said, *The answer is the lesson.* She had given Bear the riddle one evening when the temperatures had warmed again and they sat comfortably by the edge of the canal with their lines in the incoming tide.

"This is a riddle about the mystery of life," Portia had begun, and she held up a small lure. "War is the most tragic of human stories, a story of unfathomable loss. The forest fire, a tragic story of the devastating destruction of trees and animals alike. Fish die-offs—like the countless snook that froze this winter—are tragic, extinction-wary stories."

281

Portia stopped and gazed at Bear as if to say, *Are you listening?*

"But the end of the war isn't the end of that story, the extinguishing of the fire isn't the end of *that* story, and the disappearance of the killing force isn't the end of the fish die-off story either. Each storyline continues and leads to beauty, like a lead lure lost in a current that returns mysteriously golden." She held up the small lure in her hand. "How is this possible? That is your riddle." She held the lure out to Bear. "Keep this in your pocket and bring it back when you've solved the riddle."

Bear had pondered the riddle that evening as she walked home along Federal Road. She thought about it from time to time when she cut up vegetables or stirred the daily soup. She was thinking about the riddle one morning when she picked up her mail and sat at the table under the mango tree to have her coffee and sift through the small pile of envelopes. One envelope caught her attention—the return addressee, The Pelletier Group. Bear swallowed and looked around. Brandi hadn't arrived yet. She felt nervous and alone until she sensed a familiar presence next to her.

Bear sighed. "OK, Nonna," she whispered and ripped open the envelope. Bear unfolded the letter written on fine stationery and sat blinking at the words.

> *Dear Ms. Bernardi,*
>
> *We regret to inform you that, after careful considera-tion, we have decided <u>not</u> to renew your lease ending on May 1, 2009. The Pelletier Group has other plans for the space currently occupied by your café. We understand the challenges associated with moving a business and felt it most prudent to give you an extended notice of six-ty days.*
>
> *This notice does not apply to your apartment, and you are most welcome to renew that lease when it ends.*
>
> *Please feel free to contact us if you have any ques-tions.*
>
> *Sincerely,*
> *The Pelletier Group*

Bear put the letter on the table and reached for her cigarettes. She lit a clove and took a sip of cof-fee, then closed her eyes and listened to her breath-ing. The thing she had dreaded, the thing that sent her into a panic in the middle of the night, the thing that had followed her around like a dark, swirling cloud, had arrived. Maybe she was in shock. She felt almost nothing. What startled her the most was an odd sense of relief. It was the sort of relief Bear had often felt on the other side of a panic attack, when her heart had settled into a rhythmic beat again and her mind breathed and concluded that she was not in fact dying, nor had the world come to an end.

"Am I interrupting your morning meditation, Bear Bear?"

Bear opened her eyes. Linda leaned out the window of her Subaru.

"No," she said, smiling faintly.

"What's wrong?" Linda asked. She got out of her car, slammed the door dramatically, and pointed at Bear. "Are you breaking up with me?" She approached the table with one hand on her hip and the other holding a bag of pink and red Hershey kisses.

Bear laughed. "Never," she said.

"Valentine's leftovers," Linda explained, tossing the bag on the table. "Compliments of Saint Mary's pediatric unit."

"Chocolate saves the day." Bear reached for a red one.

Linda glanced at the letter under the bag of kisses.

"You getting formal love letters now, Bear Bear?"

"More like formal breakup letters." Bear handed Linda the letter and watched her face as she read it.

"Holy shit!" Linda exclaimed and looked up. "Did you just get this?"

Bear nodded.

Linda grabbed a pink chocolate. "How do you feel about it?"

"I think I'm numb."

"Anyone else know?"

Bear shook her head. "You're the first."

Linda sighed and shook her head. "You've got options, Bear Bear." She placed the letter on the table and grabbed another chocolate. "And you've got friends."

Bear smiled and nodded. She wasn't sure about the options. Opening another location would be expensive, and she just didn't have that kind of money. Would she want to, if she did? All of a sudden, every looming question was about what *she* wanted, and for the life of her, she couldn't say. But friends? That felt true. She thought of Anoki and Toni, Micki and Portia. And Linda. Linda was gold, too, she thought, just like Sophie.

"Have you heard from Sophie?" she asked.

Linda nodded and rolled the chocolate around in her mouth.

"She's in therapy twice a week now," she said. "One individual session and one with her parents."

"I'm really happy to hear that," Bear said. Sophie was going to be all right, she thought.

Linda nodded. "She's off the antidepressants. She hated them."

Bear stared out through the leaves of the mango tree.

"Sophie doesn't need antidepressants," she said. "She needs to spend time with the sea turtles again."

Linda laughed. "You know, this is the part when I usually call your weird little ass a weird little ass, but not today. Today I'm going to agree with your weird little ass."

Bear laughed. "Just don't drag her to the beach against her will," she said.

Linda's face sobered. "You know, Bear Bear," she said, "it wasn't like that on that morning." She took another chocolate and chewed it slowly, rolling the foil between her fingers. "What made it hard wasn't her resistance to go because she didn't resist at all." Linda looked up from the ball of foil. "What made it really, really hard was how much she cried and apologized. *That* broke my heart."

Bear felt tears burning behind her eyes. "That would have broken my heart too."

They sat in silence for a moment.

"I've gotta get some sleep, Bear Bear," Linda said and stood up. "Are you OK?"

Bear nodded and stood, letting Linda wrap her arms tightly around her shoulders. She needed a good, long hug. When a familiar car pulled into the parking lot, Bear's eyes widened.

"Shit," she whispered. "Ronnie just pulled in."

"Don't move," Linda whispered back and squeezed Bear even tighter.

When Ronnie's car engine turned off, Linda pulled away and held Bear's face in both hands.

"Act like you love it," she whispered and leaned in. Bear felt Linda's warm lips pressed firmly on hers and tasted the Hershey kisses, too.

After a moment, Linda pulled back and winked at Bear. "See you later, baby." She grinned broadly in Ronnie's direction and strutted toward her car.

Bear smiled and searched for something to say that might add to the show.

"What do you want for dinner?" she asked.

Linda slipped into the driver's seat and rolled her eyes. "You, baby!" she yelled out the window.

Ronnie stood next to her car, holding a large box and watching Linda drive away.

"Is that your...?" she asked as Bear walked up.

"Friend," Bear said, nodding. "She's just a friend." She looked past Ronnie to the passenger seat of Ronnie's BMW.

"Is that...?" she began.

"Isabel," said Ronnie. "She's just a friend too."

Bear tilted her head and raised her brows. "What's in the box?" she asked.

"Your mail," answered Ronnie, extending the box to Bear. "It's been piling up."

"Thanks," said Bear. She took the box, surprised by its weight.

"Some of it looks important," Ronnie said.

Bear opened the lid and looked inside. A pile of letters sat neatly on one side of the box, and on the other, a square box was tightly wrapped and taped. Bear's breath caught in her throat and tears stung her eyes. *Nonna.*

"Thank you."

"You really should do a change of address with the post office."

Bear remembered the reason she hadn't done that in the first place, but she wasn't afraid anymore of Ronnie finding out where she lived. She just didn't know where she wanted to live after the café closed next month. She smiled inwardly. The uncertainty didn't seem to frighten her as much now either.

"What's so funny?" Ronnie was asking. "Are you and your so-called friend going to move in together?"

"Why?" Bear asked. "Are you going to send another welcoming party?"

Ronnie crossed her arms. "I had nothing to do with that."

Bear smiled, which made Ronnie shift uncomfortably and blink. Bear knew Ronnie's body language. She had always known it. And she had always known when Ronnie was lying. Her own fears and self-doubt had kept her silent, but now it was a kind of game. She would count Ronnie's blinks and the number of times she pressed her lips. Ronnie's tells.

"You say that," she began, looking Ronnie steadily in the eye, "but everything points to you."

Ronnie frowned and blinked. Bear smiled and counted.

"That's crazy," Ronnie said, blinking. "Why would I do that?"

"Control, I guess," Bear said, watching Ronnie intently, counting. "Like the bank accounts and the not-so-anonymous complaints."

"What do you mean 'not-so-anonymous'?" Ronnie demanded. Her tone was angry. Her eyes held a trace of fear.

Bear smiled. *Gotcha*, she thought.

"I didn't tell you before, but Jack got drunk on New Year's Eve and told me he orchestrated that whole fake robbery," Ronnie sputtered, then pressed her lips. Tightly.

Bear imagined the New Year's scene, but in her mind's eye Jack and Ronnie commiserated drunkenly over the stunt they had planned together.

Bear laughed quietly. *Game over.*

"Sometimes I think about how much my family idolized you," she began, "and how Beth always said you were the best thing that ever happened to me." The woman standing in front of her looked smaller in stature now, as if she had deflated to the size she had always been.

"Maybe I was," Ronnie said, lifting her chin as if in vindication.

Bear nodded. "Maybe you were," she said and smiled broadly. "Goodbye, Ronnie."

"Solve the riddle yet?" Portia asked. They sat under the bridge as the sun sank in the west, turning the sky purple above them.

Bear adjusted herself on the bucket. "No," she said, irritated by the question. "I've been a little preoccupied."

"With what?"

"Is that a serious question?" muttered Bear.

Portia grinned wide, and Bear stared at the gap between Portia's two front teeth. Even the gap looked like it was grinning.

"Yes," Portia said. "What exactly are you preoccupied with?"

"My café closes for good in six weeks, Portia."

"Yes, Miss Obvious. But, I'm asking what is preoccupying your heart and mind."

Bear fixed the frown on her face and was quiet for several minutes. "The café was my dream," she said finally. "Now it's gone."

Portia nodded. "Our waking dreams are like our sleeping dreams, Bear," she said. "They come and go." She reeled in her line, checked the bait, and cast out again. "You've had many dreams. You'll have many more."

Bear was quiet again. "I don't know what I should do next or where I should go."

Portia nodded. "You're in slack tide."

Bear looked up from her pole. She knew what slack tide was, but no one had ever told her she could be in one herself.

"Slack tide is the most magical moment for the waters," Portia continued. "It appears still on the surface, but there are shifts and stirrings deep below. The energy builds until entire bodies of water move in a singular direction." She reached in her pocket, pulled out her weed pipe, and lit the bowl with a Bic lighter. She offered it to Bear, and Bear shook her head as she always did when Portia or Linda offered a smoke. "If Nonna was here—and she is—she would tell you to be still in your slack tide and listen to the stirrings of your own heart."

Bear lit a clove cigarette and smoked quietly. The first star appeared in the western sky, and she studied it for a moment. "I don't know what to do about Sophie either," she said.

"Have you talked to Nonna about her?" Portia asked.

Bear gave Portia a quick look and shook her head. "I don't discuss Sophie with Nonna."

Portia chuckled. "You two disagree?"

Bear looked away and smoked in silence.

"Sometimes," said Portia after a while, "when we love someone very much, it's hard to imagine that there may be someone better for us."

"Better than Sophie?" Bear asked, frowning. "That's impossible."

"Not a better human," said Portia. "A better match."

"I can't imagine that."

"Exactly," said Portia.

Bear woke in the middle of the night and, after tossing for nearly an hour, got out of bed and went to the kitchen to make tea. The full moon shone brightly through the balcony windows and reflected off the picture of Nonna. Bear sat on the sofa and stared at the large box on the coffee table. She hadn't wanted to face Nonna's ashes yet. Besides, she needed something pretty to put them in. She put down her tea and, carefully avoiding the small box on one side of the container, lifted the pile of mail out of the other and spread it across the table. One letter from the law firm Rossi & Rossi stood out.

Shit, thought Bear. *A collection account.* She felt a nudge to open it.

"More bad news, Nonna?" she asked. "You find this entertaining?"

Bear turned on the lamp, opened the envelope, and squinted at the letter.

Dear Ms. A. Bernardi,

Our office is attempting to reach you in regards to the last will and testament of your grandmother, Alisia Bernardi...

Chapter 16

The living room was bright with morning sunlight. The walls, though completely bare, had been freshly painted. It felt like a home to Bear.

"We haven't got anything for the living room yet," said Anoki. "We're fixing it up one room at a time." She rubbed her belly under her baggy, green overalls.

"Come see the rest of it!" Toni exclaimed.

In the center of the kitchen sat a small, wooden table with two chairs. Atop the table was a vase made from an old soda bottle, holding a few fresh, pink bougainvillea stems. Anoki and Toni's bedroom had a simple double bed with no headboard, a small dresser, and, next to the bed, a brightly painted crib.

"We got the crib at Goodwill and fixed it up," said Anoki.

Bear nodded. "You've made a beautiful home for him."

"Kai," said Toni.

Bear looked at Toni. "You've picked his name?"

"Yeah," Anoki said. "It took us a while but, like, Kai means something beautiful in five different languages."

"The sea," said Toni.

"Peace and harmony," said Anoki.

"Guardian of earth," added Toni. "My favorite."

"Kai is a perfect name for your son," said Bear. Toni and Anoki stood hand and hand in their empty living room and beamed.

"We're going to miss Les Beans so much, Bear," Anoki said.

Bear smiled. "Me too," she said. "But I'll still be around, for a while at least."

"You have to be here when the baby comes!" blurted Toni.

"I will," she assured them. "I promise."

"When's your last day?" Anoki asked.

"We'll close to the public on April sixteenth," she said. "Then we'll take the next two weeks to clear the place out."

"I still can't believe it," said Toni.

Bear sighed and nodded. "Thanks for showing me your beautiful home," she said. "I've got to go make some soup."

"Hey, can I get the recipe for your creamy potato kale?" Anoki asked. "That's my favorite."

Bear laughed. "You can have all the recipes you want, Momma."

Bear walked along Federal Road and under her small balcony. She smiled at the memory of that silly basket she had lowered to Sophie and wondered how long she would stay in her apartment upstairs once the café was gone. Maybe she would move to a new place—a place with a yard, or a place near mountains. These and so many other thoughts occupied her days now, like the stirrings below the still surface of a slack tide.

She rounded the corner to the café and was startled by a familiar car in the parking lot. An old Saturn wagon very much like Sophie's sat in the first space. Bear stopped and looked at the dent in the front. This was definitely Sophie's car.

"Hey!" Sophie exclaimed from the bench under the mango tree.

"Hey!" said Bear, surprised by the way Sophie wrapped her arms around her in greeting. She held Sophie tightly and exhaled.

"I'm sorry about the café," whispered Sophie. "How are you doing with all this?"

They sat close to each other on the bench under the tree, and Bear breathed in Sophie's scent—sandalwood soap, nag champa, and coffee. They had not sat this close since that frightful night on the stairs above the sea of glass, yet the memory of that night did not bring the same crushing sadness now. Bear didn't feel nervous either, like she had the night they had kissed and danced and made love. When she looked into Sophie's honey-colored, kaleidoscope eyes, she felt a sort of peace that reminded her of the way she had felt when she stood in Anoki and Toni's living room.

She shrugged. "I'd really like to believe that whole thing about when one door closes..."

"Another opens," Sophie finished. "It's more challenging to live through it."

"Portia says I'm in my slack tide," Bear said, "and I should listen to my inner shifting currents."

"Portia is a very wise woman," said Sophie. "I have a gift for you, for April Fool's Day." She pulled a card out of her back pocket and placed it on Bear's lap.

"I forgot it was April first," said Bear.

"It's the Fool," Sophie said. "My favorite card in the tarot. I think it's the perfect card for you right now."

Bear tilted her head. She didn't know much about the tarot, but she would not have thought The Fool was an auspicious card at all.

"The Fool's all about new beginnings," Sophie said. "Taking risks and having faith." She smiled. "That's you, Bear."

Bear smiled too. She looked into Sophie's eyes again, and for a fleeting moment, she saw someone else, someone familiar, gentle and wise, but not Sophie. Her mind flashed to the night she had sat at Sophie's dinner table, then flashed to the dream she had had and the woman who sat across from her. The memory of Sophie's words came back to her.

Sometimes when I look at you...

"Bear?" Sophie tilted her head. "Where did you go?"

"I... I wouldn't have guessed that," she stammered. "About The Fool."

"People who follow their hearts are often called fools," Sophie said, "but they find the gold others overlook." She picked up the card and placed it in Bear's hand. "Or maybe the gold finds them."

The large manila envelope arrived by certified mail. Bear carried it into the kitchen, placed it on the prep table, and stared at it.

"Would you like me to make you a cup of tea?" Brandi asked. "You look like you might need one."

Bear nodded. The envelope had come from the law firm of Rossi & Rossi in Boston. It contained a letter informing her of the exact amount that would be deposited into her account from Nonna's will and a letter Nonna had written to Bear before she died. The attorney had no idea what the letter said, only that the will had instructed them to guarantee its safe delivery.

"Maybe you should sit under the tree for this," Brandi said, handing Bear her tea.

Bear nodded, gathering up the envelope and her tea and stepping out of the kitchen. She wished Linda or Sophie were here. She took a bracing sip of tea and opened the envelope.

The first letter was addressed to Adelina Bernardi from Rossi & Rossi Ltd. The second envelope was handwritten, and the words brought tears down Bear's red cheeks. *To My Little Bear, Love, Nonna.* She would save that letter for last. Bear opened the first letter, and her eyes grew wide. The amount of the deposit was $13,000 and would arrive in her account any day now. Bear took a breath and exhaled.

She set aside the lawyers' letter and held Nonna's in her hands. She took a sip of tea and opened it.

My Dear Little Bear,

How I loved watching you grow! You have been my joy here in America. I know you have felt saddened sometimes by family and sometimes you have felt alone.

Please believe me when I tell you that you have family who adores you. You have not met them yet, but they know you. I have told them about you in so many letters!

When you are ready, go to them. They are waiting for you.

You must go to the village of Capistrano in Calabria. When you arrive, find Nonna Maria at the market downtown. She is expecting you.

All my love forever,

Nonna

PS Learn some Italian!

Mounds of chopped carrots, celery, and onion sat on the cutting board as Bear worked her way through a pile of fresh tomatoes for the minestrone soup. With just a few days before Les Beans Café closed its doors for good, the lunch crowd had doubled, and the afternoons stayed busy until close. Bear found herself coming out of the kitchen as little as possible in the final days to avoid the emotional outbursts of her regulars. Brandi had come up with the idea of a memory journal for customers, and they kept it on the coffee table near the couches.

"You should read some these entries, Bear," Brandi said one evening, flipping through the pages of the journal.

"I can't," said Bear. "Maybe one day."

"Have you thought of getting a Facebook page?"

"No, why?"

"It's a way of staying in touch with people," Brandi said. She held out her phone to Bear. "This is mine." Bear nodded, distracted. "You can find people too."

"What do you mean?"

"Old friends, old loves." Brandi grinned. "Would you like to find someone?"

Bear shrugged. She didn't see the point in it, but if she was curious about anyone, it would be Marabella.

"I'll show you," Brandi was saying. "Just type their name in the search bar, and I'll see if they come up."

A moment after Bear had typed the name, Brandi extended her phone. "Is this her?" she asked.

Bear glanced at the screen. There Marabella sat, on a blanket in a park with her husband and two children. Bear nodded and looked more closely. Marabella had made a beautiful family. She looked happy too. Bear felt a sense of contentment in this. Marabella was happy. That was all that mattered.

Brandi was reading the caption under the photo. "It says, 'Marabella, Rafael, and two children, Rafael Jr. and Esperanza.'"

Bear looked up quickly and absently took Brandi's phone to look for herself. *Esperanza.* She let out a gasp and felt tears fill her eyes. She squinted through her tears at an image of a little girl with eyes just like her mother's.

"She's beautiful, Bella," she whispered.

Later in the afternoon, Brandi announced from the kitchen door, "There's a reporter here, Bear. Do you want to talk to her?"

Bear stopped chopping and put the knife down. "Can you finish up this minestrone?" she asked.

"Sure. Good luck!"

"Ms. Bernardi?" The woman's voice was eager. She wore a blue jacket and matching skirt with a blouse buttoned to the top. She had painted on a bright red smile.

"That's me," Bear said.

"Sylvia Thomas with Channel Five News," she said, extending her hand.

Bear accepted it. "How can I help you?"

"Ms. Bernardi, there is an openly gay candidate for commissioner who has stated that the closing of your café is another example of the kinds of discrimination against openly gay businesses in town. He plans to take on the fight to keep your café open as part of his campaign."

Bear frowned. "I haven't heard about this," she said.

"It's actually quite exciting," the reporter gushed. "His slogan is 'Supporting family-owned businesses means all families.'" She looked wide-eyed at Bear. "And you certainly are a family-owned business that needs support!"

"My café closes in three days, Ms. Thomas," Bear said. She felt her cheeks begin to burn.

"Mr. Andretti thinks he can make a real case for your café. Go public, expose the discrimination, and keep your business open."

"Mr. Andretti has never stepped foot in my café," Bear said, keeping her voice steady.

"But you're still *family*," Ms. Thomas pressed.

Bear shook her head. It felt clear to her that this politician didn't care about her café as much as he cared about his polling numbers. "I'm not interested in being involved in Mr. Andretti's campaign."

"Well, that's disappointing," Ms. Thomas replied frankly.

Bear decided to be frank in return. "And please tell Mr. Andretti that I wish him the best, but he is *not* my family."

Micki arrived for the last open mic night with a large bouquet of roses and placed them in a vase at the corner of the stage.

"There are a lot of performers coming out tonight, Bear," she said. "These are for their farewell performance."

Bear looked around at the room and the performers and audience members streaming through the front door, the bell ringing above them. She wanted to remember every face, every sound, everything people said to her. She wanted to remember the beauty of the place. She wanted to wrap it up and take it with her on the day she closed the door for good.

Big Dan and his didgeridoo talked and laughed with Micki; behind him stood Steve the cross-dressing comic and Jason with his guitar. Pamela would read her poetry. Melissa made strange music with the static of a shortwave radio. Jenny and her sister performed step dances. Even Brandi would get on stage tonight to play bass in her three-piece band.

Debbie arrived with a white rose for Micki, then disappeared into the crowd. Anoki and Toni arrived and were quickly offered seats on the sofa, since Anoki was quite round now and her girlfriend would have given anyone the stink eye if they hadn't. Ms. Thomas from Channel Five News slipped through the door and waved at the counter.

Bear didn't expect to see Linda now that she was working nights, and so she could not suppress her joy when she walked through the door. Behind her, moving though the throng of people, bobbed a familiar wisp of red hair the color of a robin's breast.

"Sophie!" Bear gasped.

"Sophie's here?" Brandi asked, turning from the espresso machine.

But Bear had already moved from behind the counter toward Linda and Sophie. Linda wrapped her long arms around Bear's shoulders and squeezed.

"I fucking love you, Bear Bear," she said.

"I'm so glad you came!" Bear blurted. Sophie stood partly shielded by Linda, like a shy child. Her smile reminded Bear of the smile on the woman's face in her dream. Bear wondered if Sophie was overwhelmed by the crowd and the noise. Had she been in a crowd like this since the hospital?

"Hey," Sophie said, pulling Bear into an embrace.

"Hey," said Bear.

"I'm so proud of you," Sophie whispered.

"I didn't expect to see you guys," Bear said after a moment.

"We didn't think we were going to make it either," Linda said, moving to the counter for a drink. "I had planned on being on the road tonight."

"Where are you going?"

"Charlottesville." Linda practically shouted over the growing din of the room. "Been planning on this concert for months."

"Dave Matthews?"

"Who else?" Linda exclaimed.

Bear laughed. "That's awesome, Linda."

"Dragging Sophie along, too," Linda said, nodding toward their friend.

Bear glanced at Sophie, who shrugged good-naturedly.

Bear raised her brows. "That's wonderful," she said, and though she was happy that Sophie was enjoying life again, she wished she was packing to go too. Sophie must have seen it in Bear's face.

"You'll be free to go to concerts or anywhere you want very soon," she said.

When the last performer had exited the stage, Micki invited Bear up to say good night for the last time. Bear could feel the tightness in her throat as she stepped into the small pool of the stage lights.

"I'd like to thank the performers tonight for making open mic night such a magical night for all of us," Bear began. "And I'd like to thank all of you for making each day so full of new adventures, laughter, stories, and sometimes tears." Bear looked at Anoki and Toni and smiled. "It's sad to say good-bye when we've shared so much, but I know I'll carry all of this in my heart forever. I think you will too." She nodded toward Micki and Debbie. "So I want to leave you tonight, as I always do, with the words of my nonna."

She paused and glanced around the room. "Please remember, as you move through your week and all the weeks ahead, how the creator, the angels, guides, and guardians see you—the way they

308

have always seen you—that you are all so beautiful and so perfect in every way." Bear looked across the room, found Sophie, and smiled. "Thank you. I love you. Good night."

On the day before Bear would hand in her keys, she set her tea down on the coffee table and opened the farewell journal Brandi had put out for customers. The café was empty and silent except for The Weepies quietly singing "World Spins Madly On" from a speaker on the floor.

Some entries secretly professed love for someone. Some wrote about their broken hearts. Some wrote poetry or drew pictures. Many wrote thankyous for the soup, the coffee, and the love. Bear closed the journal and wiped down the coffee table. Soon, this and all the furniture in Les Beans Café would sit in homes all over town, and the kitchen equipment and prep tables would go to a local youth program.

The bell rang on the front door, and Toni and Anoki walked in.

"Did you bring the truck?" Bear asked as she embraced Toni.

"Yep," said Toni. "And a few good men!"

"I still can't believe it, Bear," Anoki said. "Our living room is going to look like the old Les Beans Café."

"I couldn't think of a better place for it," said Bear as the movers entered with a dolly. Anoki and Bear watched as they lifted and carried away the love seat, sofa, and coffee table.

"I've got one more thing for you two," said Bear. She led Anoki and Toni out to the front window. She lifted one flower box from its hooks, then another. "These are for you, Toni," she said with a shrug. "After all, they were in your dream."

During her first week without cafe duties, Bear rose early each day and walked to the bridge. Portia had insisted that fishing in the beginning of a new life was a very wise thing to do. Today, Bear had gotten to the halfway point where the bridge tender resides when her phone rang.

"How's your new life, Bear Bear?" Linda asked.

Bear pressed the phone to her ear to hear over the noise of the passing cars.

"It's quiet," said Bear. "Peaceful. I have a lot of time to think."

"You thinking about Italy?"

"Yes," Bear said over the traffic noise. "I think I'll go in a few months."

"Why wait?" asked Linda.

"I want to learn some Italian first."

"Makes sense. We have to make plans to get together, Bear Bear. I miss your weird ass."

"I'd love that!" Bear said. "Hey, how was Charlottesville?"

"Oh, man," Linda said. "I can't wait to tell you all about it. Have you talked to Sophie?"

"No, I haven't heard from her," said Bear. "Is she doing all right?"

"The family therapy has been pretty intense, but they've definitely made breakthroughs."

"That's great news," said Bear. "Well, I'm about to go fishing." She looked over the rail of the bridge and found Portia in her usual spot.

"Hey!" blurted Linda.

"Yeah?" Bear responded

"I fucking love you, Bear Bear!"

She laughed. "Love you too."

"How's it feel to be a lady of leisure?" Portia asked after Bear had walked down to join her.

Bear laughed and cast her line into the incoming current. "It's only been a week."

"Have you had enough leisure time to think about the riddle?" asked Portia.

"Yes, I have," said Bear and gave Portia some side-eye for the sarcasm.

"And?"

Bear nodded. "I think I solved it." She lit a clove cigarette and settled on her bucket seat. "The riddle presented three tragedies: war, forest fire, and great fish die-offs, each ending in death and devastation. The riddle asks, How is it possible for each story to lead to beauty?"

Portia nodded.

Bear exhaled and looked to the setting sun. On the surface of the water, all was still and silent like death, but beneath the surface, the current of creation and life still flowed, unstoppable, slowly gathering strength.

"After the war, babies were born in greater numbers than ever before, bringing beauty, love, and joy again. After the fire, seeds sprouted in the soil, enriched by the ashes, and soon the forest was greener and more lush than ever. And after a time, the waterways bloomed again with greater numbers and varieties of fish. Each story eventually led to beauty because life itself is beauty, and it's unstoppable."

Portia smiled. "Now," she said. "Apply that wisdom to *your* life."

Bear reached in her pocket and handed a small lead lure to Portia.

Portia shook her head. "Keep it till it turns to gold, grasshopper."

The next morning Bear sat on her balcony with the phone to her ear and watched the eastern sky lighten and the blooming clouds turn pink. Sophie's early morning call had surprised her.

"It's a full moon tonight," Sophie was saying. "Would you like to meet on the beach?"

"That sounds lovely."

"Like old times," Sophie said.

"Yes." Bear smiled at the memory.

"I've been wanting to talk to you," Sophie said.

"Sure," said Bear. "What did you want to talk about?"

Sophie was silent for a moment. "About new beginnings."

Bear held her breath. She remembered the tarot card Sophie had given her. The Fool. New beginnings. New love. Faith. Taking chances.

"My heart wasn't healed when we—"

"I know. It's OK," Bear murmured. This time she meant it. She had arrived at acceptance, mostly. She no longer shunned those two words Nonna had said when she had asked about Sophie all those months ago.

Different journeys.

She didn't understand all the reasons why, but it seemed that there were forces at play much greater than the gravitational pull she felt toward Sophie. These forces kept them in their own orbits, on their own trajectories. Still, if Sophie wanted to try again, would Bear abandon all warning signs, ignore any contradictory message from Nonna, and dash head-long, like some quixotic, sun-diving comet, into Sophie's beautiful sphere?

"So," Sophie was saying. "Moonrise on the beach?"

"I'll be there," said Bear, and placed her phone on her lap. She reached for her necklace and touched Nonna's ring.

"Nonna," she said to the rising golden sun. "I know you said Sophie and I..." Her voice trailed off. She wasn't even sure what she was asking. "What if things changed? Would you...?"

Bear waited and listened.

Whoever wears my ring will have my blessing.

Bear exhaled. "Thank you, Nonna."

Bear slung her camera case over her shoulders, took off her sandals, and descended the stairs to the beach next to Benny's Bar. A Rod Stewart imper-sonator in tight, shiny pants and an unbuttoned shirt sang "The First Cut Is the Deepest" and walked around the outdoor patio, crooning to the women with the most generous smiles. The air was filled with the scent of cigarettes and clam fritters.

The waves rolled in under the pier and crashed onto the beach, rumbling along the shore. Beyond the pier a few surfers waited on their boards, rising and falling with the incoming swells. *The incoming tide is roaring in tonight,* thought Bear. She peered down the beach and spotted Sophie sitting on her colorful blanket just beyond the last lifeguard station.

Sophie sat with an MP3 player on her lap, wearing earphones. She smiled when Bear approached and gestured for her to sit next to her.

"I'm listening to a perfect song for this moment," she said and handed Bear one of the earphones. "This is the song Linda said your nonna must have helped to write."

Bear put her head close enough to Sophie's to share the music. "It's 'Pyramid Song,'" Sophie whispered in Bear's free ear. "Close your eyes and listen with me."

Bear had heard the song before, but now, on the beach with the waves crashing in front of them, it sounded different. She felt Sophie's hand cover hers.

The song was ethereal, like slow dancing with the ghosts of the past. Bear closed her eyes and felt

315

herself lifted up above where they sat in the sand. Her mind traveled backward in time, back and back, through history, to places where the ocean smelled different and the air was filled with strange but familiar sounds and languages.

In her vision, Sophie's hand held hers in all of these places, their hands changing hue as time and place flashed past. Sometimes their hands were deep brown, sometimes ruddy—so many shades that matched the soil beneath them and the spices they carried. She sped backward still, through dust and smoke and the heat of fire, the aroma of bread and herbs, exotic and familiar. The shape of Sophie's hand changed, too, and the way it felt in hers. Sometimes it was a child's hand, sometimes a mother's, sometimes wide and callused, sometimes small and soft like her own. The vision returned again and again to the hands of sisters running through the thick of a forest, the driving rain of a monsoon, and the cutting winds of a frigid tundra; through a crowded street; and into the waves of an ocean.

Bear opened her eyes and looked at Sophie rocking gently to the music, her eyes closed, still traveling. And Bear saw Sophie with new eyes, eyes that held the wisdom of the dusty roads they had traveled, the fires they had tended, the languages they had spoken. And Bear saw in Sophie's face what Sophie had seen in hers the night she had sat at Sophie's table. Sophie, too, was ancient and familiar.

She is family. Nonna's voice was soft, like someone who had placed a gift on a child's lap.

Bear saw the truth of it in Sophie's hand. The memories that had been carried forward on every scent and sound now filled her senses. The rosemary so present in Sophie's sauce and in the little clay pots on her sill. How had she not seen the mirror of Sophie in herself? Bear felt as though her heart might crack open and surrendered, instead, to tears.

My sister. My twin.

Bear lifted Sophie's hand and looked through blurred eyes at the mark just above her wrist. In the place that had once been cut open in despair, a small tattoo of a baby sea turtle covered the scar. She traced the tattoo with her fingers and her salty tears. *My twin.*

Sophie had been watching her and squeezed her hand. She wept too.

"We found each other," Sophie said. "Again."

Bear tried to speak, but her face pinched against her words.

317

"Do you remember the dream you had the night we spent together?" Sophie asked, wiping Bear's face with her hand.

Bear nodded.

"Did you ever figure out who the woman was?"

"I thought maybe it was the spirit in the tree."

Sophie smiled. "And the others?"

"I don't know," Bear said. "Do you?"

"They were family, Bear," she said. "All of them."

Bear squinted toward the crashing waves.

"Even her?" said Bear.

"Yes."

"That's why she wouldn't ..."

"Yes."

Bear shook her head. "I really loved her." She looked at Sophie again, and her eyes widened.

"Was she...?" Bear whispered.

Sophie smiled, and they sat in silence, under the roar of the waves and the darkening hues of twilight above the ocean.

"Did you ever talk to Nonna about us?"

Bear nodded toward the ocean.

"What did Nonna say?" asked Sophie.

"Different journeys." Bear sighed. She had been so blind to it and so stubborn.

Sophie nodded.

Bear shook her head. "I was such a fool today," she said. "I thought I had finally accepted what Nonna was trying to tell me about us, but after you called I started doubting what I'd do if you asked me to..."

Sophie's laugh caught Bear by surprise, but before its sting could register, Sophie said, "You're not the only one Nonna talks to, Bear. We'd both get quite a scolding."

This time Bear laughed out loud. Of course, she thought. In some mysterious way, Nonna belonged to Sophie too.

"There is someone I want to talk to you about, though."

Bear's eyes grew wide. "Someone?"

Sophie nodded and turned to the boardwalk behind them. Bear followed Sophie's gaze to a figure waving from the steps.

Linda.

Bear looked at Sophie again and could not hide her surprise.

"You and Linda?"

Sophie nodded and chuckled, a flush rising in her cheeks. Bear's thoughts raced back to that terrible night when Sophie almost ended her life. To

Linda's steady and protective presence. To her courage to make the most difficult decision, even if it meant Sophie might hate her for it. She let out a quiet laugh as the realization came to her. Far from Sophie hating Linda for what she did that day, Sophie most likely fell in love with her. Bear knew this as sure as she knew herself. She would have fallen in love, too.

"She's perfect, Sophie." Bear squeezed Sophie's hand and turned toward the boardwalk again. Linda walked in long strides toward them and Bear sprang to her feet and ran toward her friend. This time she threw her arms around Linda's neck.

"It's perfect," she whispered. "*You're* perfect!"

"I fucking love you, Bear Bear," Linda said.

The moon peeked over the horizon, and Sophie stood and pointed.

"Here it comes!" she shouted.

"It's so beautiful!" Bear said, her voice filled with the kind of wonder she had had the morning she watched the baby sea turtles.

"There's something we need to do, Bear," said Sophie, taking Bear's hand.

"Oh, boy," said Linda. "Brace yourself, Bear Bear."

Bear looked from Linda to Sophie.

"We need to swim into it," Sophie said. "We need to swim into our new life."

Bear's eyes widened at the rumbling, crashing waves and the golden moonrise just beyond.

"OK," she said and swallowed.

She and Sophie stood at the water's edge and looked into the roaring mouth of the ocean.

"You can do this," Linda said, just behind them.

Sophie nodded and squeezed Bear's hand.

They ran, as they had before and before, clinging to each other, into the wild waves. The first towering wave lifted Bear and threw her backward under the weight of the water and pulled her with the surging tide toward shore again. Saltwater stung her nose and filled her mouth; sand scraped skin from her arm. Sophie's hands tugged at her shirt, her arm, and grasped her hand again, pulling her toward the waves and the rising moon. Another wave rolled over them, and this time Sophie fell away, tossed and tumbling toward the shore. Bear found Sophie's outstretched hand and pulled her up again, gasping. The salt stung Bear's mouth, her throat and eyes, and blurred her way ahead.

When they had pulled themselves past the breaking waves and floated on the rolling hills of the ocean, Sophie pulled Bear to her until their brows touched.

"We did it, Bear," she said, her face and mouth dripping with water.

Neither Sophie nor Bear knew that Linda stood at the water's edge with the lens of Bear's camera pointed at the full moon.

Bear nodded. "What now?"

Sophie laughed. "We ride the waves home."

Weeks later, when Bear scrolled through the old pictures she had taken of soups, coffee, couples, and performers at Les Beans Café, she would find the picture Linda had taken the evening she and Sophie had swum into their new lives—a silhouette of the two of them in the golden glow of a rising moon. Two sisters, in an embrace, touching souls. She would see its likeness in the sign that had hung above her café and wonder if this image had been there all along, drawing her, pulling her into an un-stoppable current, a current that had always been there, moving her toward an unfathomable, unfold-ing miracle, pulling her with a firm and invisible hand into the heart-cracking joy of reunion, across a perilous and beautiful universe.

Epilogue

2009
Three months later
Capistrano, Italy

The Mercedes traveled southeast along Strada Provinciale, from the airport in Lamenzia Terme through rolling, green hills scattered with old olive trees and stone farmhouses. Bear lowered the window a little so she could breathe in the air of Calabria. The air, or something in it, stirred Bear's whole being, reminding her of the times when, as a child, she had stood still in Nonna's kitchen on Sunday afternoons, breathing in the aroma of her grandmother's special herbed bread, made with olives and rosemary. A mysterious anticipation had ignited in her the moment she placed her foot on this soil, breathed the air, and felt the kiss of Mediterranean sun on her skin—as if she had returned to an ancient home. Everything was new, and everything was familiar.

Bear had learned enough Italian in the last few months to be able to thank the driver and ask him what she owed in Italian. They had driven slowly down a narrow street and arrived at a small market set apart on the street by its green door. The driver pointed, nodded, and smiled.

"Ecco qui!"

Bear placed her hand on The Fool's card and the picture of baby Kai, which had both rested on her lap during her journey by air and again as she approached Capistrano. She tucked them into the side pocket of her travel bag and reached into another pocket for Nonna's letter. She stepped out onto the quiet, stone street of the village and breathed in the air, a mix of floral scents with cooked sweet onion and herbs. *I'm here, Nonna,* she whispered.

The small, green door opened, and Bear smiled at the sweet familiarity of a small, brass bell ringing above her head. She stepped into Nonna Maria's market, and a wave of aromas washed over her, filling her senses. Rows of herbs, red peppers and prosciutto hung from the ceiling. Wheels and wedges of cheese filled display shelves. Baskets of bread, some long and some round, filled wooden shelves. The scent of fresh herbs floated through the room around the hanging meats and cheeses. Thyme, basil, oregano. The scent of rosemary rose above all the rest, turning Bear's head as if to follow its scent to some hidden memory.

A small, spectacled woman appeared behind the counter, barely tall enough to see over the top.

"*Buongiorno*," Bear said in her best Italian accent.

"*Salve*," said the small woman and walked around the counter to stand in front of Bear.

"*Mi chiamo—*" Bear began.

"*Orsa?*" asked the woman. "*Sei Orsa?*"

"*Si*," Bear said. "*Mia nonna...*"

"Alisia!"

"Si."

The little woman's arms flew open.

"*Stavamo aspettando!*" she said, announcing how long the family had been waiting for Bear's arrival in Italian.

Her small, chunky arms wrapped around Bear.

"Alisia told us everything about you! We saw you grow up! Come with me. I want to show you something. Here you are! Here you are!" Nonna Maria's Italian was fast and excited. She spoke too quickly for Bear to understand every word.

Nonna Maria had already grabbed Bear's hand and was leading her to a small room behind the counter. She pulled the chain on a lamp and illuminated an office with a desk. A calendar hung above the desk and, to the right of the calendar, a corkboard with a collage of pictures. At first Bear thought they were pictures of the woman's family. Maybe there would be a childhood picture of Nonna and Nonna Maria, Bear thought. Nonna Maria pushed Bear closer to the corkboard display. "Ecco! Ecco!"

Bear leaned closer and squinted at the photos until her breath caught in her throat and her eyes became a stinging blur. The pictures had been arranged in chronological order: baby pictures, elementary school pictures, high school, college. A picture of a high school graduation brought Bear's hand to her mouth to stifle a sob. These pictures, every last one of them, followed Bear from infancy through high school and to the last picture Bear had sent Nonna in her nursing home. Every picture Bear had given Nonna, Nonna had sent on to Nonna Maria. Bear looked at the graduation picture. How proud Nonna had looked to stand next to her on graduation day even in her wrinkled, purple graduation gown.

"Cosi preziosa," Nonna Maria whispered. "So precious." She turned to leave and patted Bear on

the back. "Are you hungry?" she asked in her own tongue. "I have bread and cheese and coffee and ham..."

"I will have all of this," Bear replied in her awkward Italian. "*Grazie!*"

"Tomorrow you will go and see the others," Nonna Maria continued to speak in Italian from the counter. She brought down a log of prosciutto and put it on a cutting board. "Oriana will accompany you."

Bear sat at a small table as Nonna Maria cut the bread, prosciutto, and fresh mozzarella. She sipped the espresso Nonna Maria had placed in front of her and wished she could call Linda and Sophie. How she wished she could share every minute of this.

Nonna Maria placed a plate on the table with fresh-cut bread, thin slices of prosciutto, mozzarella, olives, and a small glass of red wine.

"*Gustare!*" she exclaimed and patted Bear on the shoulder. "Così preziosa!"

When Bear had finished eating, Nonna Maria sat down across from her.

"I have a room for you upstairs," she said. "I'll show you now." She took Bear's hand and gestured for her to come. "You have to rest."

Nonna Maria led Bear to the back of the shop and up a narrow stairway to a rooftop living space and a small bedroom with a single bed and chair.

"This room is your room," she said, speaking more slowly now. "Tomorrow Oriana will pick you up at noon."

Bear nodded. "Grazie, Nonna Maria."

"*Dormi bene*," said Nonna Maria and closed the door.

Bear sat on the small bed and fell back on the soft pillow. She breathed in the cool air that flowed through the window and listened to the motion and melodic voices on the street below. Soon she had fallen asleep in her travel clothes and boots, holding Nonna's letter to her heart.

"Poverina!" Nonna Maria said, standing over Bear's bed. "You slept in your clothes."

"Si, Nonna Maria," Bear said sleepily, raising herself on one elbow. "I fell asleep so fast." She sat up in bed as Nonna Maria opened the shades and placed a clean towel on her bed. "I slept well, though."

"Molto buona!" Nonna Maria exclaimed and patted Bear roughly on the back. "Venga! Mangiare!"

Bear washed quickly and came down the narrow stairs, following the aroma of fresh coffee and baked sweets. On the small table by the counter,

Nonna Maria had placed a small cappuccino and biscuit.

"Mangiare!" she said again, and pulled the small chair back. "Oriana will be here soon."

"Grazie, Nonna Maria." Bear sipped her cappuccino and took a bite of the biscuit. She closed her eyes and savored the sweetness on her tongue. This, too, tasted like home.

Nonna Maria was in joyous spirits and danced and twirled around the store, humming a song Bear did not recognize, then disappeared into the back office. Moments later, Luciano Pavarotti sang "Nessun dorma" from a scratchy turntable record, his voice moving elegantly around the hanging prosciutto and baskets of bread.

"Balla con me, Orsa!" Nonna Maria sang and gestured to Bear.

"OK, Nonna Maria." Bear awkwardly stood to accept her invitation, remembering a night not so long ago when Linda had shouted the same invitation, in English, from the tiny stage of Les Beans Café. Nonna Maria took Bear's hands and moved around the room in a part waltz and part Maypole dance that made Bear laugh so loudly and so completely that her belly ached.

"Brava! Brava!" a voice shouted over the music. Nonna Maria stopped with her arms midair and looked toward the door.

"Oriana!" she called.

Bear stood, breathless and blinking at the woman in the doorway. Oriana was a stranger, but everything about her seemed familiar. Her wild, dark hair reminded Bear of Toni. Her oversize overalls reminded her of Anoki. Oriana's red Converse high-tops reminded her of Micki. And when Oriana smiled broadly, exposing a wide gap in her two bright front teeth, Bear thought of Portia. Oriana wore a long, gemstone necklace that held a single yellow feather. She was a collage of the friends who had led Bear here, who had put her on the plane and waved goodbye.

"Buongiorno, Orsa!" Oriana approached, ignoring Bear's outstretched hand. She embraced her instead, wrapping her arms tightly around Bear's shoulders. Every embrace Linda had ever given her was in Oriana's arms.

"Buongiorno, Oriana," Bear said, and though she could not take her eyes off of the woman, she felt awkward under her steady gaze.

"Sorry, but you are so beautiful," Oriana said in a dialect different from Nonna Maria's. She smiled broadly. "You are more beautiful than your photos."

Bear felt her cheeks flush and remembered how awkward she had felt when Sophie had called her beautiful.

"Hai visto le mie fotos?" asked Bear. Had Oriana seen the photos in that office too? The baby pictures and that embarrassing graduation picture in her wrinkled gown? Bear felt another flush of embarrassment.

"Yes," Oriana said. "And I speak a little English too."

"Oh!" exclaimed Bear.

"I went to university in London." Oriana said, nodding proudly.

Nonna Maria came out from behind the counter with a ceramic casserole dish covered in a cloth.

"Devi andare adesso!" she said and put the dish in Bear's hands. "Do not be late."

"What have you prepared?" Oriana asked and peeked under the cloth, her eyes widening at the warm cheese tart, powdered with white sugar, that she found there. "Pastiera napoletana!"

"It smells so good," said Bear.

"Andare! Andare!" Nonna Maria nudged Bear and Oriana toward the door.

"Do you know where we are going?" Bear asked once they were out on the stoop.

"Of course!" said Oriana with a laugh.

That makes one of us, thought Bear.

Oriana's scooter was parked just outside the door, and Oriana slid onto her seat, moving forward to allow ample room for Bear behind her.

"You will have to hold on with one hand and hold the pastiera with the other," she said. Bear climbed on the scooter, putting one hand lightly around Oriana's waist.

"Are you and I related, Oriana?" asked Bear.

Oriana laughed. "No," she said. "I am a Morelli, but everyone else you will see is a Bernardi."

"May I ask you one more thing before we go?"

Oriana turned off the engine and turned to face Bear. "Of course!" she said, her deep brown eyes smiling in anticipation.

"What is that feather you wear?"

"You like my feather?" Oriana asked, smiling widely and touching the yellow feather on her necklace. Bear nodded and felt a blush rising in her cheeks. Everything about Oriana disarmed her. Her deep, brown eyes, rich and warm like the soil of a spring garden. Her sun kissed cheeks, which re- vealed a constellation of tiny freckles that Bear could see now with Oriana's face so close. Her body exuded a kind of earthy strength that tilted Bear's senses toward her, and her skin, the subtle scent of an unfamiliar cologne with hints of wood and tobacco. "This feather is very special," Oriana began, "because it is a sparrow's feather and sparrows are very special birds."

"Why?"

"Well, it is our country's bird, the sparrow, but I like it because of the magical sparrow in the Cenerentola story."

"What is that?"

"In America, it is Cinderella."

Bear felt a pang of disappointment. "Cinderella?"

"Yes!" Oriana exclaimed. "You know it?"

"The story about a neglected girl who is saved by a prince because she fits a slipper and they all live happily ever after?" Bear's heart sank as she said the words.

Oriana turned to face Bear and shook her head. "That is not the Italian story. In the Italian story, Cenerentola is smart and strong and knows magic. The sparrow is her beloved friend and does magic too."

Bear laughed. "A magic sparrow?"

"Oh, yes!" Oriana exclaimed. "And Cenerentola carries the sparrow next to her heart always." She touched the feather on her necklace and smiled.

"I'd like to hear that story," Bear said, relieved. She settled into her seat behind Oriana, extending her hand again lightly around her waist.

Oriana pressed Bear's hand more tightly to her and started the scooter. They rode east out of town along a winding road with rolling hills on one side and mountains in the distance on the other. The air was full of the scent of earth and greenness and blossoms. Bear did not recognize any of the scents she breathed in, and yet they seemed familiar.

Their scooter traveled farther into the countryside, past little stone homes where women bent in gardens, past old men on bicycles, past rows of ancient olive trees. Everything, thought Bear, everything about this place — the fragrant air, the sunlight on rolling hills, the men and women and even the feel of Oriana's strength—felt like home.

Suddenly, somewhere above the din of the scooter, Bear heard Nonna's laughter— the kind of laughter that had filled the kitchen long ago whenever Bear tasted Nonna's cooking and her eyes widened with wonder and delight.

They veered south down a secondary road and finally came to rest on a dirt driveway in front of a humble stone farmhouse. Oriana hopped off and extended her arms.

"I can carry the pastiera," she offered.

"Where are—" But Bear was interrupted by shouts and applause, which came from the farmhouse porch.

"Brava, Orsa! Brava! Brava! Brava, Orsa!"

Startled, Bear looked to Oriana.

"Why are they applauding?" she asked.

Oriana laughed. "They are applauding because you have come!"

Bear shook her head and looked up to the porch, teeming with strangers, waving, clapping. Her thoughts spun backward to a dream. Men with dark, curly hair and ties. Women in flowery dresses with children in their arms.

"Are they...?" Bear asked.

"Your family," Oriana said, in a tone that reminded Bear of Sophie's voice when she said, Remember who you are. Remember your name.

A wave of dizzying emotion made Bear sway where she stood and reach for something solid to hold.

Oriana stepped back and held out her hand.

"Don't worry, mia amate," she said. "I'll be your sparrow."

Acknowledgements

There are so many people for whom I am deeply grateful. I am forever blessed to have made the acquaintances of so many beautiful souls while operating a certain little seaside cafe. Some have been fictionalized in the pages of this book.

A big thank you to my amazing editor Jessica Hatch and to my cover designer, the very talented Ashe Rodriguez.

A special thank you to the Beta readers for taking the time to read a pretty rough first draft and give valuable feedback.

And a special thank you with so much love to my dear friends who supported this endeavor from the very start.

Most of all, I'd like to thank you, the one reading this because maybe you've come to the end of the book and you've just kept going. Thank you for inviting the cast of characters in *Perilous and Beautiful* into your home and heart.

Much Love to all of you,
Patti

If you would like to cook up some of the soups and breads mentioned in *Perilous and Beautiful,* you can get a copy of *Wildflowers and Wooden Spoons.*, a cookbook with recipes and stories from Mother Earth Cafe.

You may also like *Wildflowers and Present Tenses*, my memoir.

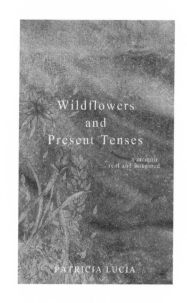

Next in the Sea Turtle Series ...

Orsa and Oriana
(2024)

Their story picks up with "I'll be your sparrow" but what oceans must they cross to be together? What challenges rise like gale force winds? And what secrets wait in the dark waters below? The quirky and lovable characters from *Perilous and Beautiful* come together again for friendship and love.

Let's stay connected!

Visit my website and sign up for my quarterly newsletter. Stay updated on my upcoming books and get discounts!
Just scan the QR code!

Made in the USA
Middletown, DE
19 March 2023

27112882R00203